Handmade with Love

Rachel Bowdler

Books By This Author

Partners In Crime

Paint Me Yours

The Secret Weapon

Saving The Star

No Love Lost

Holding On To Bluebell Lodge

Along For The Ride

Dance With Me

The Fate Of Us

The Flower Shop On Prinsengracht

The Divide

Content Warnings

Health problems such as dementia and stroke

Sexual affairs and other marital and familial problems such as poor parenting

One

Stevie usually enjoyed the comfort of rainy Welsh summers by the sea, but after the twelfth consecutive day of staring out of the Little Shop of Driftwood's shell-decorated windows, even she was beginning to tire of the dreary weather. It wasn't bringing in any customers, for starters, and also made it all the more unpleasant to comb the beach for supplies. So far this week, she had collected nothing more than a few green shards of an old wine bottle, which she brushed the sand off now to make... What? She didn't know.

Her weary huff ended with her head bowed in her hands. The entire store was filled with all sorts of carved driftwood ornaments and wall hangings, but recently, Stevie was running out of new ideas.

It was difficult to make anything at all when nobody was buying, anyway. With the tourists warded off by bad weather and the last few arts and craft markets cancelled for the same reason, Stevie's profits were dwindling at an alarming rate. It was something she had put off admitting to herself after a fairly decent spring, but her financial struggles were no longer something she could push to the corner with the rest of the old, rotting wood and useless, cracked sea glass.

And even if she could, her hostile landlord, Deirdre, would surely not let her forget that she was behind on rent once again.

Rising from her seat, Stevie gave up on her creation and drifted through handmade wind-chimes and baby mobiles to swap the Open sign on the door to Closed and lock up. Since she clearly wasn't needed here, she may as well have an early lunch and perhaps check on her father.

After shrugging on her yellow raincoat and looping her purse across her shoulder, she pushed through the dangling beads dividing the store's threshold from the back hallway, shivering against the balmy draught sifting through the poorly insu-lated back entrance. Maybe going out wasn't such a good idea, but she was starving and craving one of Paddy's sausage and bean pasties.

Just as she was about to plunge herself into the pelting rainfall, a series of clatters and bangs caused her to startle. She turned, ready to greet the new tenant of the apartment above. Deirdre had warned that there would be an arrival earlier in the week, but the landlord hadn't warned Stevie of who it was.

Stinging recognition sliced through her at the sight of the brunette woman standing on the stairs, hauling a human-sized suitcase to the first floor. Stevie knew her. She knew her too well, in fact. She had run her fingers through those damp, dark curls once upon a time, had kissed those heart-shaped lips, had held those rain-reddened hands....

As shock tore through her, Stevie readied her hand on the door handle for a quick exit... But it was too late.

Anna, Stevie's ex-girlfriend, the very woman who had shredded her heart to ribbons she would spend her life trying to sew back together, turned her gaze to Stevie midway through a grunt of exhaustion.

Her blue-grey eyes, the same shade as the ocean thrashing outside, widened with realisation, the rosiness draining from her cheeks in the same instance. With the distraction, Anna's grip on the handle of the suitcase loosened, and the luggage toppled down the stairs without warning. It landed at the toe of Stevie's Etsy-bought huarache sandals. Stevie could only stare at it and try to force the damp, humid air into her lungs.

"Oh, barnacles!" Anna cursed, covering a hand to her mouth.

Stevie was glad to see the woman still refused to use actual swear words, as though she was a nursery school teacher and not — well, Stevie didn't actually know what Anna did anymore. The last she'd heard of her was through their mutual friend, Levi, who had told her that Anna had graduated from Cardiff with a degree in politics. She'd never returned to their small village of Castell Bay after that, not even for Levi's wedding or to visit family over Christmas.

Until now.

Lips pursed and face burning, Stevie shifted away from the suitcase and avoided meeting Anna's eyes. "Tell me..." Her mouth was dry. She swallowed and tried again. "Tell me you're not the new tenant moving in upstairs." It was almost a plea.

"No. I just felt like hauling everything I own up and down the stairs for the exercise."

Stevie only realised then that there were, in fact, a dozen different boxes piled beneath the staircase. It didn't feel like a promising sign, and she didn't feel like sticking around to bear the brunt of any more of Anna's cutting sarcasm, especially not when her heart began to pound ferociously in her chest.

"Well, enjoy."

"Wait!" Anna called, skipping down the steps two at a time until she was closer. Too close. Stevie had to fight the urge to confirm it was Anna: that her ex-girlfriend, the former love of her life, was indeed standing at the foot of the stairs in the back entrance of her store.

How? Why? Stevie had never expected to see her again. It was easier to forget her that way. She only thought of her now twice a week, tops, which had dropped dramatically from when she had thought of her every waking moment of every day. And that strained muscle always snagging in her chest after their confusing, heart-wrenching

4

breakup? That had healed to nothing more than a tough bit of gristle she could easily ignore. But not if Anna continued to stand in front of Stevie, narrowed eyes glittering and brows drawn together.

"What?"

"Is that it?" asked Anna. "Is that all we're going to say to each other?"

Stevie didn't know *what* to say. Her day had been boring and uneventful as of five minutes ago. Now she could barely breathe. "I'm sorry I didn't prepare a welcome wagon. You might want to warn me next time."

Why hadn't Stevie been warned? If not by Anna, then by *someone*. Levi, at least, who she knew still kept in contact with Anna. Surely they would have told her about something this important. Surely she deserved that.

"Yes, well, I didn't think *you* would be the first person I'd see the minute I got back into town," Anna snapped churlishly, crossing her arms over her chest.

"Right," Stevie scoffed. "Why would you see me *here*, in the back entrance of *my* shop?"

Anna paused at that, a flicker of surprise passing over her annoyingly perfect features. Even now, eight years since the last time Stevie had seen her, pixelated on a Skype call, she looked no different, no older. Stevie probably did. She was well aware of the weight she'd put on since her teenage years, and she'd chopped all of her red-gold hair off so that it fell just above her shoulders. Not to mention the permanent stain of purple beneath her eyes, a result of too many sleepless nights and early mornings.

"*Your* shop?" Anna asked.

"*My* shop," Stevie confirmed. "You didn't know? Levi didn't tell you?"

"I…." Anna worried at her lip, all of her confidence and hostility seeming to diminish until she was just… Anna. Until it was difficult for Stevie to look at her without remembering road trips through Welsh valleys, drunken nights on the pier, cold water lapping against bare skin, slurping raspberry slushies through a shared straw, and a weightless, unbridled joy that Stevie had never been able to find anywhere else.

"I haven't spoken to Levi yet."

Stevie's face crumpled with a puzzled frown. "Oh."

"Only because I know they'd make a huge fuss and I'm just trying to settle back here… well, quietly."

"You don't owe me an explanation." It felt like a lie. Anna had owed her plenty of explanations, really, after the way she'd ended things — over a call where she had made it clear she just couldn't do long-distance. She hadn't even asked Stevie why she had dropped out of university to come home. Their split had come out of nowhere, and Stevie had spent the next few years wondering just how long Anna had wanted to break things off but hadn't been able to find a good enough excuse until Stevie had given her one.

It had broken her.

Anna had broken her.

With the memory, Stevie straightened as though a decent posture might protect her from feeling that way again. She wouldn't show Anna any dreg of vulnerability, even if she *was* on the brink of collapse from the scent of that familiar rosy perfume alone, made all the more pungent from the rain.

"I should go," said Stevie finally, flipping up her hood and preparing herself once again for the merciless downpour outside. She suddenly longed to be caught in it; longed to be anywhere but here.

"Stevie," Anna replied, and Stevie's name on her tongue... her knees almost gave out at the sound. So long. It had been so long. And yet it somehow felt as though no time had passed between them at all. As though Stevie was still that loved up nineteen-year-old desperate for Anna's touch.

"I'd like to talk to you about this," Anna said. "If I'm going to be living above your store, I don't want any animosity between us."

"There's no animosity between us. There's nothing at all between us."

"Really?" Anna arched a perfectly plucked eyebrow.

"Really." Stevie nodded, doing her best to gulp down the acid burning her throat. "It's ancient history."

Worrying her lip, Anna hesitated, and Stevie tried not to squirm away from her sharp scrutiny. "Okay. Then I suppose it was nice to see you."

Stevie couldn't find it in her to say the same, so she only forced a tight-lipped smile and escaped into the rain, letting the door shut behind her.

Her words should have been true; it should have been ancient history. But as she made her way to Paddy's Pies on the seafront, wind buffeting through her thin coat, it didn't feel like ancient history. It didn't feel like history at all.

Because Stevie had never gotten a goodbye, an apology, an explanation. She had been abandoned and forgotten by a woman she'd thought she could trust. And now Anna was back.

Stevie didn't know quite what to do with that.

∞∞∞

The bell above the shop door tinkled for the first time at three thirty that afternoon, long after Stevie had taken to having a nap at the counter. Well, she had tried to, at least. It was difficult to silence her mind long enough when she knew that the sporadic creaking of floorboards from the ceiling above was the cause of Anna Conway's expensive black loafers.

Anna had at least stayed clear of Stevie for the rest of the afternoon, though Stevie had heard her trampling up and down the stairs with boxes often enough. When Levi wandered in with the twins, then, Stevie perked up, schooling her features into a cheerful mask.

It's not their fault, she reminded herself. *They didn't know.*

"Auntie Stevie!" Lois and Ralph at least sported wild smiles as they bounded through the shop, nearly knocking over half of Stevie's stock in the process. Chocolate framed Lois's mouth like a moustache, and Ralph sported a pink strawberry one to match. Levi had treated them to ice creams, then.

"Look at you two mucky pups," she greeted, rounding the counter and crouching with outstretched arms. The twins rushed into them, nearly sending Stevie toppling in the process. "Where's *my* ice cream?"

"Baba ate it!" Ralph accused, pointing a grimy finger towards Levi. As a nonbinary parent, Baba was the label they'd chosen for themself with the help of their husband, Quentin. It had also been one of Lois's first words, and they had decided that the title was perfect for Levi.

Stevie gasped feigned disgust now, shooting a glare Levi's way.

"This is not what we discussed, kids," Levi chastised. "We made pinkie promises to keep the ice cream a secret from Auntie Stevie *and* Daddy."

Stevie smirked, ruffling Lois's dark curls as she stood. "After the day I've had, I need lots of ice cream. I'm hurt you didn't bring me any."

"Uh-oh," whistled Levi. "Should I put the kettle on and pull up a chair?"

"Maybe," Stevie said, though they would find it difficult since there were no kettles and only one chair in the store.

There must have been something telling in Stevie's expression because Levi's own features turned grave, their inky eyes searching.

"Hang on." They pulled out a pack of wet wipes and cleaned the ice cream from the twins' hands and faces quickly. "Why don't you two monkeys go and play with the dollhouse while I talk to Auntie Stevie?"

They did, scurrying over to the farthest corner of the store where Stevie's pride and joy lay. Other than the twins, though, nobody else showed so much as a lick of interest for the dollhouse Stevie had made of driftwood and old fabrics. It was the most expensive piece in the store, mostly because it had taken her months to complete, and she loved the rustic details and tiny furniture so much that part of her was glad nobody had come to take it home. Some things were worth more than profit.

"What's going on?" Levi asked when the kids had disappeared, their thick brows knitting together in concern. "Is it your dad?"

"No, he's fine." Stevie busied her hands by reorganising the set of postcards on the counter, provided by Marigold in exchange for Stevie's wall plaques. "When was the last time you spoke to Anna?"

Levi pondered the question, burying their hands into their pockets. "I don't know. A couple of months ago, maybe. Why?"

"Because... " Stevie pointed to the ceiling, where she could still hear Anna shuffling in the room above, "she's upstairs."

Levi's eyes widened, mouth parting. "*No*."

"Yes," she hissed through gritted teeth. "She moved in this morning."

Stunned, Levi lifted their gaze to the ceiling as though they could see straight through the bricks and mortar separating them from Anna's new home. "Did you know she was coming back?"

"No. It was a very unpleasant surprise to find her standing in the stairwell earlier."

"Why wouldn't she tell anyone?" Levi wondered. "I mean, I get why she wouldn't talk to you, but... me? Her best friend?"

"Oi! You're *my* best friend."

"I'm *both* of your best friends. There's enough Levi to go around."

"Well," scoffed Stevie, "only *one* of us bothered to turn up to your wedding — as maid of honour, might I add — *and* offers free babysitting services. And I *still* get no ice cream!"

Glassy-eyed, Levi appeared not to be listening. "What did she say to you, though? Was it all romantic? An old flame returns and you lock gazes for the first time in eight years and realise...."

Stevie rolled her eyes. "It was awkward and uncomfortable and confusing. We most certainly did not lock gazes." They had, but she didn't feel like telling Levi that and risk another romantic monologue of how they'd like to think the whole thing went. "She didn't know my shop was under her apartment, apparently. I didn't stick around to have much more of a conversation than that."

As she said it, the sound of footsteps traipsing back down the stairwell echoed through the store. A dimple sank at the corner of Levi's mouth, a scheming smirk unfolding on their lips. "Is that her?"

"Don't, Levi —"

"Anna!" Levi called through cupped hands. "Anna Conway! Is that you?"

Sighing, Stevie pinched the bridge of her nose. "Why?"

"I only want to see my old friend." They batted their thick lashes innocently. Stevie knew now where Lois had gotten her doe-eyed 'no-I-didn't-smear-your-lipstick-all-over-the-white-bathroom-wall' look from.

"Then see her somewhere else!" Stevie snarled irritably. "Believe it or not, I don't fancy seeing my ex-girlfriend — the woman who broke my heart — twice in one day."

"You're having some tough luck then," Levi muttered under their breath, inclining their head to something past Stevie. She whirled, and her heart flipped up into her throat for the second time that day at the sight of Anna. Only now, dread accompanied it too. How much of Stevie's barbed words had her ex just heard?

"Do my eyes deceive me, or is Anna Conway back in Castell Bay?" Levi pulled Anna into a tight hug before she could answer, and Anna let them reluctantly. She had never been one for any sort of public displays of affection, even with Stevie. It came from a difficult childhood with an emotionally stunted mother — another reason Stevie was surprised that Anna was back at all. Her parents still lived on the other side of the village. They were bound to run into her sometime soon. "Why didn't you tell me?"

"It was a last-minute decision," Anna murmured, pulling the hem of her blouse down uncomfortably when Levi pulled away. "I was going to call you tomorrow."

"I'm sure," Levi nodded, unconvinced. "What brings you back?"

"I got a job for the council, actually. The opportunity and pay were too good to pass up, so I start tomorrow."

"Fancy. Well, now you're here, you have to meet my little ones."

"Of course, you're a parent now! Congratulations!"

Levi thanked her and guided her past Stevie to gesture to the twins, who were too enthralled by their wooden dolls to notice Anna at all.

Stevie couldn't help but shake her head in

disapproval. How could Levi call Anna a friend when she'd never even met their children? Stevie had been there every step of the way, from the adoption to middle-of-the-night fevers and hospital runs to now. They'd been in Levi's life for three years, adopted when they were two, and Anna couldn't have dragged herself back from Cardiff to show an interest in them even once?

"And you have to come to my graduation party next weekend!" Levi continued, casting a pointed, sidelong glance towards Stevie. She only glared back and tidied the counter with stiff movements, the boxes of sea glass clattering noisily.

"Oh." Anna's eyes flitted hesitantly toward Stevie. "Maybe that's not a good idea. I don't want to make anybody uncomfortable."

"Nobody's uncomfortable, Anna," Stevie forced out, smoothing down her skirt and drying her sweaty palms in the process. "Well, I'm not, anyway."

"Come on. I never got to celebrate graduation at the same time as you." Levi dug their elbow into Anna's ribs. "*And* you didn't come to my wedding. You owe me."

Anna shifted on her feet, throat bobbing as she swallowed. Stevie pretended not to notice when her grey eyes fell back to her a final time, as though she was asking for Stevie's permission.

She wouldn't get it.

"Okay then." Anna smiled tightly. "I'll be there."

"Good. We have so much catching up — *Ralph!*" Levi's attention sharpened on their son, who was bopping his sister with a giant conch from one of the shell racks. "Put that down and stop abusing your sister!"

"But she stuck a pencil in my ear!" cried Ralph with a pout.

Levi scoffed and lifted the twins from the floor, prying a pencil from Lois's hands. Stevie didn't know where the child got it from. Stevie didn't even *sell* pencils.

"Alright, let's go home before you drive me barking mad. Come on. Say bye to Auntie Stevie and Auntie Anna."

"Bye, Auntie Stevie!" Ralph shouted at the same time that Lois mumbled, "We don't have an Auntie Anna."

Stevie tried to suppress the smugness she felt at that, waving as Levi and the children left while Levi still lectured them calmly. A ringing silence descended with their departure, and Stevie tried to fill it with the rhythmic taps of her chewed fingernails on the counter.

"I never thought I'd see Levi with kids," Anna said finally. "And this place... it's lovely, Stevie. How long have you had it?"

"Four years." Stevie couldn't bring herself to answer in any more detail than that.

Anna nodded, fingers brushing across a lighthouse ornament Stevie had chiselled from driftwood and then painted glossy reds and whites. "You were always so creative. I knew you'd do something great with it all."

Hearing her talk that way about Stevie, as though Anna knew her down to her very core, made Stevie feel sick, and she had to squeeze her eyes shut to calm her ragged breathing. It took every fibre in her not to scream and shout and tell her to get out. "Thanks."

"I'm sorry I didn't tell you," Anna said finally. "That I was coming back, I mean. I should have."

"What you do is none of my business. It's fine."

"Stevie —"

"I think I'm going to close up early, so... bye." Stevie locked up the cash register with so much force the key almost broke, and then organised the shelves with trembling fingers behind the counter. When she straightened again, Anna was still there, still staring at her.

She opened her mouth as though about to say something, and Stevie's stomach lurched with anticipation — whatever it was, Anna clamped it down. "Alright. I'll get out of your hair, then."

Anna made a swift exit, leaving Stevie to breathe a sigh of relief in her absence.

Stevie had never been able to breathe around Anna — once, it had been because of something pleasant and warm and all-consuming, now only pain clogged her airways.

But Stevie would get on with it. She would

be fine. She always was.

And she had faced far worse things than this before now.

Two

It had been a long first week back in Castell Bay. Anna had spent most of it hiding either in her apartment or her new office in the town hall in order to avoid bumping into her parents. She knew it was wrong; had prepared herself for the inevitable reunion as soon as the job of policy and economic development advisor had been offered to her in her hometown. But there would never be enough time to prepare for her mother. She had barely kept in contact with Jen at all over the years. They had never really gotten along, and there were things about her mother that Anna could not find it in her to forgive yet.

It was made worse by the fact her ex-girl-friend worked below Anna's apartment. Luckily, the store closed as she was on her way home, usually after having taken a detour to avoid running into Stevie at the back exit of the building. Still, seeing her for the first time after so long of trying to forget her... it had pulled Anna out of her own skin and left her feeling stripped bare. With those piercing hazel eyes, Stevie had always had a way of doing that: shredding through Anna's defences with ease and finding what lay beneath. No matter how guarded Anna was with everyone else, she had never been able to hide from her.

And finding Stevie waiting for Anna at the bottom of the staircase that first day... It had felt like coming home, somehow, in a way nothing else had. She had driven past piers where she'd spent every summer running up and down as a child, had returned to her favourite ice cream parlour and walked by the old primary school she'd attended, but that nostalgia was nothing compared to Stevie's red-gold hair, floral trousers, and the freckles splattered across her nose that Anna had tried to make constellations out of when they should have been studying.

It shouldn't have felt that way, Anna knew. She had chosen to walk away — to *run* away — from Castell Bay and everyone in it. It had been years since she had last seen or heard of Stevie, and even Levi knew not to mention the woman's name around Anna on the rare occasion they found time to catch up. So why had seeing her again left Anna's mouth painfully dry, her heart fluttering its way out the slats of her ribs?

Why had she not stopped thinking of it since?

Whatever the answer may be, Anna tried to push it away as she wandered across the beach, the heels of her black pumps sinking into damp, pebbled sand. Her first mode of action was to protect the thing she had always loved most about Castell Bay, and that was the coastline. So, she had spent the morning handing out flyers informing tourists and locals alike of the new protection on shells, sea glass, driftwood, and anything else people usually liked to take home from the beach as a souvenir. It was a surefire way for word to get back to her mother about Anna's return, but there wasn't much to do about that now.

Besides, she realised, eyes narrowing on a hunched figure a few metres away: she had a beachcomber to shoo away.

Anna had to dodge a yapping poodle at her ankles to reach the offender, almost tripping over its retractable lead as the uneven stones crunched beneath her feet.

"*Brutus!*" its owner scolded before glancing at Anna apologetically. "Sorry, love. It's not you he's after. He's chasing the seagulls."

Oh, what a relief I'm not about to be mauled by your poodle. Anna tried very hard not to glare and continued on to the beachcomber.

"Excuse me!" she shouted as she reached them. She couldn't tell much about them in the blinding sun other than the fact they were likely a woman, with an oversized, floppy sun hat and a floral dress that rippled in the briny sea breeze. Ignorantly, the perpetrator continued to shovel up and sort through handfuls of shells, throwing the ones she must have thought worthy in a wicker basket that already contained a fair amount of driftwood pieces.

"Excuse me," Anna repeated, words lost over

the whistling wind and the poodle's barking once again. Impatiently, she sighed and tapped the woman's shoulder. "Excuse me."

The beachcomber straightened and turned, and an icy wave of dread rushed through Anna's veins. Hazel eyes. Freckled skin. Choppy strawberry-blonde hair whose curling ends brushed a softly-rounded jaw.

Stevie.

At the sight of Anna, Stevie's features hardened, and she slung her basket onto her arm expectantly. "Yes?"

Though it was a warm day, Anna almost shivered against Stevie's frosty reception. She couldn't remember ever being the subject of it before. Stevie was always the kinder, pleasant one when they were younger; sunlight made flesh, both inside and out. Apparently, a lot had changed — or she just really hated Anna, which was fair enough. Anna had broken up with her suddenly and without discussion to protect herself from the long-distance difficulties they would have otherwise faced.

"Sorry." Anna chewed on her bottom lip and scraped her dark hair from her face, into the wind. "I didn't realise it was you."

"Surprise, then," Stevie sang through a sarcasm-laced melody, brows knitting together as she adjusted her straw hat. Her eyes remained dark in its shade: murky and unwelcoming. Anna no longer wanted them to bore into her.

"Can I help you?"

Anna pushed any desire to shrink aside, though, instead tilting her chin and straightening her spine. *Professional*, she reminded herself. *Be professional.*

"Unfortunately, I have to ask that you put the driftwood and shells back on the sand. Castell Bay's council have just introduced a new bylaw protecting any materials from being taken from the shore."

A bitter scoff fell from Stevie. "You can't be serious."

Anna passed her a glossy flyer, lips pursed into a flat, *very* serious line. "As you can see, anybody who fails to comply with the new rules will be fined one hundred pounds."

"But I use them for crafting!" Stevie argued. "Everything in my shop is made from things I pick up on the beach — and you know that."

Apologetically, Anna shrugged and tried not to acknowledge the guilt bubbling in her stomach. She had known that, but she hadn't thought she'd see Stevie collecting things on the one day Anna was trying to spread awareness of the issue. "Then I'd suggest finding another beach. It can't be one rule for you and another for everyone else."

"This is ridiculous. *You're* being ridiculous."

"I'm protecting our beach under very valid bylaws," she explained, guilt evaporating to make way for slow-burning anger. She was being civil, and yet Stevie was anything but. Even with their history, it was childish and only made Anna's job harder.

"But half of this stuff is debris!" Stevie motioned wildly to the driftwood jutting from the basket. "Sea glass and driftwood —"

"Actually, driftwood isn't debris at all," Anna interrupted. "There are plenty of living species found in that wood, and you're destroying their habitats."

Stevie sneered at that, crossing her arms over her chest and, as a result, dragging the neckline of her summer dress even lower. Anna made a special effort not to let her gaze fall below Stevie's neck, though her new curves had left Anna's breath clogged in her throat the first time she'd seen her, even when covered in an oversized raincoat. Stevie seemed to hold herself more confidently with them: no longer a teenage girl, but a woman. A beautiful but infuriating one, at that.

"My entire business relies on these resources, Anna. You can't just change the law because you feel like it."

It was the first time Anna had heard Stevie speak her name since her return, and it struck through her bones like the hourly chime of the town hall bells. It was so familiar and, yet, so completely new. She didn't know how to react as though hearing it hadn't left her shaken and raw.

"If you have an issue, you're more than welcome to raise it with the council in the next meeting on Friday. Until then, you'll have to leave your collection here. Otherwise, I'll have to give you a fine, and despite how it may seem, I really don't want to do that, Stevie."

A muscle in Stevie's jaw ticked. With her blazing eyes trained unwaveringly on Anna, she tipped up the basket and let the shells and wood fall at their feet. "Happy?"

Pasting a false smile on her face, Anna kicked away a shell that had fallen on her foot and nodded. "Thank you."

Stevie opened her mouth to say more, but Anna never found out what it was. A fat, white droplet plopped on Anna's shoulder pad. Anna pulled at the pinstripe grey fabric to see what it was and found an obscenely large splatter of sea-gull faeces staining her expensive new suit. *Barnacles*. What had people been *feeding* them?

A stifled chuckle caught in Stevie's throat, causing Anna to send a cutting scowl her way. Above them, the gulls circled and squawked as though laughing proudly at their practical joke. *Bastards*.

Stevie only shrugged. "You know what they say. Muck for luck."

"Hilarious," Anna deadpanned. "Do you have a tissue?"

"I think there's a new law against removing natural materials from the beach. I'll see you at the council meeting, though." Stevie smirked and whirled around, sandalled feet crunching away from Anna, away from the beach.

Irritation smouldering within her, Anna glowered at the retreating figure, then examined her soiled jacket a final time.

She regretted it almost immediately and set off herself in search of something to wipe the droppings away. She just hoped it would come out in the wash.

"Ruddy seagulls," she muttered, shooting daggers up to the bird-riddled sky. "I'm protecting your habitat, and this is how you repay me?"

Laughter-like croaks and falling white feathers were Anna's only reply.

Stevie had not set foot in Castell Bay's grand town hall since the age of ten when she had made the mistake of joining the school choir and was forced to compete with a song she could neither understand nor pronounce the lyrics — mainly because they were all in Welsh, and she had never bothered to learn her country's dying language.

It was a little bit different marching into the meeting room as an adult with a bone to pick for the elderly council she had once felt shy performing for. Anna was the only one without silver hair and age spots, and she sat in the corner of the mosaicked collection of tables, eyes gleaming with just as much irritation as yesterday. Despite her own frustration, Stevie had to clamp down a laugh at the memory of bird crap landing on her shoulder.

Karma's a bitch, and so are British seagulls. It might have been petty but Anna had deserved to be knocked down a peg or two after her absurd threat of a one-hundred-pound fine. All for a bit of bloody driftwood that would only wash back into the sea otherwise.

Apparently, Stevie was not the only local with complaints either. The cluster of chairs was filled with familiar faces, and she had to sit through all of their rants and raves before they reached her. Marigold, the woman who ran the souvenir shop on the seafront, was sick and tired of dodging dog poop on her way to work and petitioning for fines to be enforced on the pavements as well as the beaches. Paddy, the best pastry maker in the village, claimed he was always late on deliveries because of potholes on the roads. Edna, an eighty-year-old, spent her time playing devil's advocate for the sake of something to do with her Friday afternoon, baiting the others into heated arguments about why nothing was ever done. It was all very riveting.

And then Stevie raised her hand when asked if there was anything else to address, and with Councillor Ernie's permission, she stood and cleared her throat. She still clutched the leaflet Anna had given to her yesterday in her sweaty hands.

"Thank you, Ernie." She bowed her head and

smoothed down her skirt, pretending not to notice Anna crossing her arms in her peripheral vision. "I'm here today to contest the recent ban on removing materials from the beach. As most of you know, I run the Little Shop of Driftwood on my own and make all of my handmade goods with driftwood, sea glass, seashells, and anything else I can find lying about. It's never posed a problem before and the tourists love everything I sell, especially because they're made with recycled materials. Being threatened with a fine if I continue my business causes quite an issue for me and my livelihood."

"I see." Ernie nodded sympathetically. "It is Miss Conway who is in charge of our new bylaws regarding the Coast Protection Act. I have to admit I didn't realise this would be an issue for our locals. As you can imagine, it was put in place with tourists in mind."

"Which I understand perfectly," Stevie agreed. "But, unfortunately, Miss Conway's bylaws are also affecting my business. I was wondering if there might be a way around it."

"Miss Conway?" Ernie gestured for Anna to come forward, and she did, chair scraping against wooden floorboards as she stood.

"So, to get this straight, Miss Turner," she said with her nose snootily jabbing the air, "you wish to be the only person in Castell Bay to be excluded from our bylaws? You think you are owed a privilege nobody else in the village will be offered?"

"That's not what I'm asking at all." Stevie tried her best to keep her voice calm, steady, as she stared her ex-girlfriend down. It felt as though she was in the middle of a court hearing for a crime she didn't commit. The problem was trying to convince the jury of it too. "I am asking you to rethink the ban for the sake of local business owners who rely on sourcing these materials."

"Does anybody else here know of anyone who benefits from destroying coastal wildlife habitats?" Anna asked.

Nobody raised their hand. Not even Edna, who had been so vocal throughout the entire meeting. Apparently, the devil no longer needed an advocate.

"That hardly seems fair," Stevie ground out. "Two thousand people live in this village. Only twelve of them are in this meeting. Ernie. You've known me my whole life and have said yourself how wonderful my gifts are. You buy your wife's birthday presents from me every year! Don't you have something to say about this?"

"Well, uh," Ernie stammered hesitantly, scratching the whiskers on his chin.

"Miss Turner, might we suggest that you look into a business venture that does not come with the risk of harming our ecosystem?" Councillor Judith piped up: a stony-faced, stern-voiced old woman with round glasses perched on her long nose. "I worked with Miss Conway on these bylaws and am absolutely certain they are a positive way of addressing an issue that has long since plagued our beach."

Red splotches smattered Stevie's cheeks as her anger intensified. This was her business. Her livelihood. The only thing she had ever been proud of or had the opportunity to pursue. Anna had been in town less than a week and had ripped it from her. "So that's it, is it? The council is no longer interested in protecting their village's small businesses?"

"It isn't the matter of small businesses," Anna said. "It's the matter of our coastal habitats. As Judith pointed out, if your business poses a direct risk to that, it sounds like you may want to think of more eco-friendly ways to go about your work."

Stevie shook her head, a brimming kettle about to reach boiling point. "This is ridiculous! What if a child pinches a shell to take home in their pocket because they don't know any better? Will you give them a one-hundred-pound fine too?"

"One shell is not the same as the basketful of materials you collect."

She huffed, swiping her sweaty bangs from her face and pinching the bridge of her nose.

"It's not personal, Miss Turner," Judith said. "But it is necessary."

But it felt personal. Stevie's eyes blazed as she glared at Anna, tasting venom on her tongue.

Why had she come back? Why had it taken less than a week for Anna to ruin everything Stevie had built?

Why?

"If it's so necessary, it wouldn't only be coming into effect now," she said. "I've been running my business for four years and never once heard anybody in this room or out of it raise the issue of protecting habitats. Never."

"I'm with Stevie on this one," Marigold chimed in, standing from her seat and casting a small smile her way. Stevie breathed a sigh of relief, though she had expected as much. Marigold was one of her best customers and always ordered in bulk for her own shop. "I've purchased a lot of Stevie's stock for the souvenir shop, and the tourists love it. It adds character to our stores, our village. You can't pull the rug from under her so suddenly when it's never been a problem before."

"Well —" Judith began, but Ernie silenced her with a raised, wrinkled hand.

"Alright, let's put it to a vote, shall we?" he proposed.

Hope fluttered in Stevie's chest. She was among friends. People she'd known all her life. But then there were the sour-faced council members before her thinking they were more important than they were. They didn't care about Stevie's business.

Please, she tried to beg them with desperate eyes.

"All those in favour of lifting the recent Coast Protection Act, raise your hand."

Stevie, Marigold, Paddy, and Kirk, the local butcher, did — and one councillor who Stevie knew to be friends with her mother. The rest remained still as stone and just as craggy-faced. Stevie sighed, eyes fluttering shut in defeat.

"All those in favour of enforcing the ban long-term?"

She didn't need to look to know the outcome. Whatever Anna had done this last week, she'd clearly won herself some followers.

"I'm sorry, Stevie," Ernie spoke softly, dabbing his shiny forehead with an embroidered handkerchief. "All issues can be revisited again in six months, though. Perhaps we might reconsider then."

Stevie swallowed the lump in her throat, unable to look anywhere but at her feet as she sat down. Fortunately, hers was the last discussion to be had, so she made a quick getaway. She was one foot out of the town hall when a voice pulled her back.

"Stevie!"

She knew who the voice belonged to. She just had no interest in turning back to see its owner's face. So, she continued out of the arched doorway and onto the cobbles of a village that no longer felt like hers.

∞∞∞

A larger Etsy order had left Stevie working late that night. She didn't mind. She thought too much when she went home, worried too much about her father, and that meant that she fussed over him until he lost patience. Better she was here, painting beneath the silvery light of her desk lamp, the vicious wind rattling the doors, and a soft melody floating from her Spotify playlist.

Until the beads and shells tinkled to life behind her. So used to being alone, she jumped and almost smudged the red paint across her driftwood-carved lighthouse. Almost. The steadiest thing about her was her hands, and she dropped the paintbrush just in time.

It was Anna who lingered sheepishly in the threshold, decorated by common cockles and periwinkles bleached by salt and sun. The curtains were the first things Stevie had ever made, with only string, beads, sea glass, and shells to go at. "You're working late."

Stevie scowled and went back to painting. "Before you give me a fine, I collected these before the ban."

"Are you sure? Do you have proof?"

She arched an eyebrow, finding that Anna's lips quivered with a smirk. "You're hilarious."

"I didn't mean for this to affect your business, Stevie."

"Well, it did." She kept her eyes trained on the delicate strokes of her brush, even as Anna drew closer, bracing her palms across the counter.

"It's beautiful."

With a huff of frustration, Stevie threw her brush down again and wiped her paint-stained fingers on an old rag. "What do you want, Anna?"

Anna frowned. "I saw your light on and wanted to explain myself."

"I don't mean *now*. I mean why are you back in general? To make my life more difficult?"

"I'm back because I got a good job here," she snapped. "It has nothing to do with you."

"Good. Then let it stay that way, please."

"I didn't think we had a problem."

"We didn't!" Stevie winced against the crack in her own voice, hoping that Anna wouldn't hear the pain bleeding through, pain she had never quite been able to heal. "Until you decided to enforce a ban that stops me from being able to run my business properly. That's a problem for me, Anna."

Anna's expression remained smooth, unreadable. A ship bobbing distantly on the horizon, always slightly out of reach. Stevie supposed she had always felt that way about Anna. "There's nothing I can do about that now."

"Clearly," Stevie scoffed. The truth was, she had enough supplies to at least see her through the month. But after that? She had no idea. The closest public beach bar Castell Bay's was forty minutes away, near Aberystwyth, and Stevie didn't have a car. Even if she did, there weren't nearly enough materials washed up there to make it worth her while. Everything she'd built here had been built around this beach, this village, and Anna had taken it all away without so much as a warning.

Anna sighed now, shoulders slumping and head bowed as though she was trying to meet Stevie's gaze. Stevie refused to cave. "Look, it's Levi's graduation party this weekend and I don't want this to ruin it for them. Can we please just be civil?"

It was easy for Anna to ask that of Stevie. She hadn't been abandoned and rejected and heartbroken. She wasn't struggling just to keep her business afloat. She wasn't living with a constant, stifling weight pinned to her chest with all of the things that needed doing, fixing, making. And in the dim light, with the wind howling outside and Anna staring at her so oblivious to it all, Stevie almost let it break her then.

Almost.

But she was stronger than that, stronger than what Anna had done to her both then and now, so she gulped it all down and breathed through the pain as she said, "Fine. No problem."

Three

Anxiety jittered in Stevie's stomach as she stepped into the Fat Ox. The pub was already crowded with Levi's friends and family, colourful bunting strung along the top of the bar with letters that spelt, 'Con-grad-ulations!' Apparently, Quentin, Levi's husband, had convinced the grumpy landlord to decorate for the special occasion — but then, that wasn't surprising. Everybody loved Quentin. He was the most charming person in the village. That meant he could convince anybody of anything.

Maybe he can convince Anna to stop being an arrogant arsewipe, Stevie thought as she rose to her tiptoes in search of Levi. They were nowhere in sight, but the back door leading to the beer garden was open. A good job, too. Humidity had blanketed Castell Bay seemingly overnight, and the back of her dress was already damp and clinging to her skin with sweat.

She saw no sign of Anna either, and hoped that her ex hadn't arrived yet — or at all. After ordering a Pimm's that was more lemonade than gin at the bar, she was cornered by Levi's family and friends into conversations about the weather and her father's wellness and, "You know, Arnold has been selling deformed, two-headed potatoes in his farm shop! Can you believe it?"

Stevie could not believe it. She couldn't find it in her to care, either, her gaze sliding past Gwen's silvery bob every now and again to make sure Anna wasn't around as she nodded with feigned interest. A Bon Jovi song roared above the din of conversation, and it almost felt too much. It had been a long time since Stevie had been in such a crowded, noisy space.

Luckily, Quentin's grinning face floated over the sea of heads like a smiley-faced balloon set loose. His warm features brightened as he caught sight of Stevie and waved before approaching.

"Hello, my love." He hauled Stevie into a tight hug, and Stevie couldn't help but smile into his cologne-drenched shirt. "Levi's been looking for you."

"I'm running late," she nodded apologetically as she pulled away. "My dad."

Concern lined Quentin's forehead. "Is he alright?"

Stevie nodded, though she wasn't sure. She didn't think he had been alright for a long time, and now dementia chipped away at him day by day. It had started after his stroke — that was when Stevie had dropped out of university to help her mother care for him until he got back on his feet. But he never did, not without his family and a pool of treatments and healthcare. Depression tore through his recovery, and just as things started to get better, the dementia diagnosis came.

It had been like this for Stevie ever since: late to events because Jack needed help showering or he felt ill or Bryn, her mother, couldn't cope any longer. If it wasn't Levi's graduation, something they'd been working towards for eons and always felt bad about accomplishing later in life than their friends, she wouldn't have turned up at all. She only spent time away from the house worrying and feeling guilty.

"Where's your other half, anyway?" Stevie asked in an attempt to change the subject. She dangled the recycled, sparkly gift bag clutched in her sweaty palms in front of Quentin. Half of the glitter had transferred to her dress already. "I have their gift."

"Let me sneak a peek!" Quentin peered into the bag, face splitting with a smile and cheeks dimpling at what he found. "They'll love it. Come on, they're outside."

He pinched Stevie's elbow and guided her out into the gardens, where it was only a little bit less stuffy and crowded but still reeked of bitter ale — and everybody seemed significantly more drunk. Levi stood in the centre, dark hair braided and chin cleanly-shaven. Happy. Anna leaned against them, laughing at something Levi's younger sister, Tamsin, was saying.

Stevie stopped, feeling as though she had swallowed a nest of wasps. She wasn't part of this. Hadn't been even before Anna's return. How could she be? She was always working or taking care of Jack or Bryn or just trying to keep herself in one piece.

She could never stand there with her friends, laughing without a care in the world.

"You alright?" Quentin asked, his hand squeezing Stevie's shoulder. "I can't believe she's back after so long. Have you talked?"

"A little." She shrugged and sucked in a breath, swallowing down her Pimm's for extra courage. If Stevie could go head to head with Anna in the town hall, councillors and locals watching, she could spend one night pretending to be a normal person who laughed and danced and got drunk, for Levi's benefit if not her own.

So, she plunged into the crowd, weaving through earsplitting conversations and spilt drinks that left her bare arms sticky until she reached Levi, Anna, and Tamsin.

"Stevie!" Levi cheered when they noticed her, pulling her into a vodka-laced hug. "I was about to call you!"

"Long time, no see, babe." Tamsin grinned. They had always gotten along — she and Tamsin — mostly over their shared aunt duties with the twins.

Anna only nodded her greeting, and Stevie pretended not to notice.

"Sorry I'm late." Stevie had to shout to be heard over a raucous peal of laughter behind her, the current slowly nudging her towards the fairy light-covered trellis. They hadn't been illuminated yet, with amber sunlight pouring through the high fence. "I brought your gift."

Levi's eyes lightened eagerly as they took the gift bag and searched its contents. They pulled out the card first, a handmade sketch featuring a champagne bottle, and then came the gift: a graduation cap made of driftwood and sea glass, painted and adorned with a golden tassel. She had hooked a string to it so that it could be hung on a wall, and her signature 'handmade with love' had been stamped with metallic ink beneath.

"It's just a little keepsake to show how proud I am of you." Stevie shrugged, her cheeks heating beneath everyone's attention. Tamsin let out an "*aaaaaww*" as it was passed around. "I know how hard you worked."

And they had. Levi was a mature student after struggling with anxiety through their teens and then taking time to figure out what they wanted to do in their early twenties. Finally, after meeting Quentin, they had set their heart on teaching; soon, that would be their full-time job. Stevie had been there through all the university applications and decisions, through personal statements and student loans and proofreading essays. She knew how much this meant because it had meant a lot to her once, before she'd left. She'd studied history and archaeology — Stevie didn't know why or what she might have become, but she could imagine it being something fancy.

She'd have to wear smart clothes every day and work in different places, rather than the paint-stained, threadbare overalls she wore now. Then, she hadn't needed to think past university. She'd enjoyed history and had been with Anna and had shared a dorm room with people she had liked. Everything had been perfectly unplanned.

But it felt too late for all of that now, even knowing it hadn't been for Levi. And she loved the shop. She loved creating things to sell. It was just a shame it was slowly draining her of any money.

"I love it," Levi said, placing a soft kiss in Stevie's hair. "Thank you."

"You're welcome." Stevie forced a smile despite the tears pricking her eyes, feeling odd when she noticed Anna watching. It was the first time they'd really all been together since Anna left. She sipped her drink — a fancy pink cocktail with sugar lacing the rim of the glass — with magenta-painted lips and manicured nails.

"Isn't it lovely, Anna?" Levi asked, displaying the ornament pointedly.

Anna nodded politely. "Very."

"Isn't Stevie very, very talented?"

Both Stevie and Anna glared at that. It was typical of Levi to play mediator. Any normal person would ignore the fraught tension.

"She certainly is," Anna agreed finally, grinding her teeth.

"Make the most of it," Stevie couldn't help but add, though she knew it was petty. "I'm not allowed to use driftwood anymore to make your gifts."

"What?" Levi's brows furrowed. "Why?"

Anna huffed and threw back the last of her cocktail. "I need another drink. Anyone else?"

She didn't hang around to catch the answer, shoving past Stevie and the rest of the guests until she disappeared. Stevie shook her head bitterly, drawing her gaze back to Levi. Their face was still crumpled with confusion.

"What was that about?"

"Nothing." Stevie shrugged, picking at her chipped, burgundy nail polish as a belated wave of shame took hold. This was *Levi's* night. It wasn't about her or Anna, and she shouldn't have made it such.

Levi pinched Stevie's freckled arm until she winced.

"*Ow!*"

"Spill!" they ordered.

"Fine." Caving, Stevie sat down on the outdoor couch and placed down her drink on the table. Levi followed, resting their head in their hand to show they weren't going to drop it.

"Go on. What have I missed in Stanna land?"

"*Stanna*?" Stevie raised a brow.

"Stevie and Anna. Stanna." When Stevie only blinked blankly, they huffed. "Come on! I gave you that ship name years ago!"

Stevie rolled her eyes. "We don't need a ship name. It sank years ago. If anything, we should be called *Titanic*."

"Uh-huh," hummed Levi without sounding convinced. "Sure. So, go on. Why no driftwood?"

"Because our dear councillor Anna is enforcing a new bylaw against it. The Coastal Protection Act or something." Stevie batted away the words with her hands, lips downturned sourly. "I even went to that bloody council meeting yesterday to try to contest it — a complete waste of time, by the way. Judith Barlow got all snooty and sided with Anna."

"Are you telling me that you had a whole courtroom drama with Anna yesterday and didn't invite me to watch?"

Stevie could envision Levi now, stuffing their face with popcorn while Stevie battled for her business.

"I wish you wouldn't enjoy this so much," she grumbled.

"Oh, come on." Levi reached for her hand, lacing their fingers with hers. "I can't help it. You're like Ross and Rachel. Everyone knows you two are supposed to be together in the end."

"Right." Stevie scoffed, wrinkling her nose at the thought, not only because she hated the comparison to the *Friends* couple — who had taken far too long to stop messing around and get together, by the way — but also because it was not the least bit true. "That's why we haven't spoken in eight years."

"You were on a break." Levi smirked at their

own joke. "She's back now."

"And ruining my business," Stevie pointed out. "How romantic."

They cocked their head knowingly as though Stevie was one of the twins getting up to mischief and due for a scolding. "Have you even spoken to her? Like, *really* spoken to her?"

"I don't *want* to speak to her." Stevie plucked the sliced orange from her Pimm's if only to combat the foul taste in her mouth. It only fueled her bitterness in the end. "I'll be civil for your sake but that's where it ends."

Levi rolled their eyes. "Stubborn as mules, the both of you."

"I vaguely remember you ignoring Quentin for a week when you first started dating because he forgot that you don't like tomatoes and ordered you a Margherita pizza."

"And look at us now." Levi beamed, rising from the chair and letting their fingers dance across the fine blond hairs dusting the nape of Quentin's neck. Quentin was in mid-conversation with Tamsin, but still caught their hand and laced their fingers together. It made Stevie ache. Levi could romanticise Stevie's turbulent, now non-existent relationship with Anna all they wanted, but Stevie and Anna would never be in love again. And Stevie would probably never have that love with anyone else either. The relationship had ended long ago.

Ancient history that kept being dredged up.

Ancient history she desperately wanted to forget.

"I need another drink. Want one?" Levi offered.

"No, I'm good," Stevie said, swallowing her pain.

"Tough. It's my graduation party and I say you're having another. Tamsin, keep her company."

Tamsin did, sitting beside Stevie while Quentin joined her on the other side. Good. At least if Anna came back, she was sandwiched between two shields.

∞∞∞

Perched on a barstool, the stale stench of beer stinging her nostrils, Anna twirled her umbrella solemnly around her cocktail glass and pretended the drink tasted as a cosmopolitan should. If there were cranberries in it, they were most definitely from a carton and diluted by water. The fact didn't stop her from gulping the last dregs in one go, leaving sugar crusting her lips that she promptly licked off.

A good job too. Levi sidled up beside her a moment later, ordering a screwdriver. It was met with nothing more than a grunt from Helen, the pub's grumpy landlord. Anna supposed she was less than happy about the confetti and spilt beer she'd have to clean up on account of Levi's party later.

Ignoring the owner's foul mood, Levi jabbed a finger into Anna's ribs. "I hope you're not moping at my graduation party, Anna Conway."

"I'm not moping," Anna replied, though she was perhaps moping a little bit. She had underestimated how difficult it would be to see Stevie again after so long, and it only seemed to get worse each time they ran into each other. The fact Anna's new bylaws, which were supposed to be a positive thing, were threatening her business didn't help either, but there was nothing to be done about that now. Why should she have to choose between protecting habitats and appeasing her ex-girlfriend?

"Stevie told me about your whole 'battle of the beach' thing."

"Ugh," Anna groaned, massaging her throbbing temples. "Great. I suppose you think I'm awful too."

"No." Levi's drink was placed in front of them, and they slurped it through their reusable straw slowly. "I think your flirting tactics need some polishing."

She frowned, bewildered. "What? I'm not flirting!"

"You're not flirting, you're not moping." Levi rattled off on their fingers. "What *are* you, then?"

"I'm…." Anna stuttered, the question leaving her dumbfounded. *What* was she? Uncomfortable. Confused. Perhaps still a little bit attracted to Stevie, but unless she'd had some vital transformation in their time apart, that was to be expected. It wasn't as though they'd split up from a lack of love. Anna wished they had.

She couldn't see past that. Couldn't separate each thread of emotion knotting through the roiling mess in her gut. Returning to Castell Bay was always going to be difficult, but she'd never expected it to be living-above-your-ex's-store, banning-her-from-collecting-driftwood-on-the-beach-while-a-seagull-shits-on-you difficult. Not to mention the way she'd been skirting about town to avoid her parents. One drama at a time was quite enough for Anna.

She crushed the paper umbrella in her hands. "I'm enjoying your party."

"Look, I'm trying to be Switzerland here because you know I adore you both, but... you hurt Stevie a lot when you broke up with her."

"I know." Anna didn't like to think about that conversation: the one they'd had over Skype. There had been no goodbyes. No closure. But Anna hadn't had a choice, even if she hadn't truly wanted to leave Stevie behind. Stevie was her person, her partner, the fire to her ice, and Anna had loved her ferociously and without apology. She hadn't had that before or since. She couldn't let herself.

And in all that heartbreak, she hadn't been able to think about where it had left Stevie. What kind of hurt Anna had wreaked on her. She couldn't. She had been selfish because it was the only way she knew how to be.

But she doubted she could keep ignoring her regrets forever. Not now, when Levi was looking at her as though she'd spiked their drink with vinegar, brows drawn together and dark eyes glittering with the expectation of an explanation.

Anna didn't have one. Not one that was good enough.

"And no matter how you pretend, I know it hurt you, too," they continued.

Anna refused to admit that truth. She scowled at the swirling sugar in her cosmo instead.

"You never told me why," Levi said when she didn't reply.

"I never told *her* why either." Anna wiped her sweaty palms on her pleated trousers. "I don't have a good reason. I know you're fishing for one because you're our friend, and you want us to rekindle something so it can be like it used to but... that won't happen. Sorry."

"Anna." Levi reached out and placed their hand over hers. It was cool and damp from the condensation dripping on their glass. And then they gave her that 'Levi look', the one Anna had never been able to resist. They were like a Labrador, with round eyes and a small pout and that guaranteed, somehow, that her secret was safe with them. That they understood. "You can tell me."

Chewing on her bottom lip, Anna tried to remain strong against that look. "There's nothing to tell."

"*Anna*."

And she caved. Of course she did, because the secret had been brimming inside her for eight years, and perhaps she just wanted *one* person in this village to not look at her as though she had done something terrible. "I just couldn't come back here, okay? Not then. It didn't feel like I had any choice but to break up with her."

Levi's expression twisted, puzzled. "Why?"

"*Because*. You know I never got on with my parents."

"Yeah, but you tolerated them and so did Stevie."

"Well, I stopped being able to tolerate them when I walked in on my mum having sex with the postman."

The noise around them seemed to dull, though perhaps that was just the pulse in her ears muffling the rest of the world to murmurs. Even so, the confession might as well have been blurted on a stage into a microphone for all the embarrassment and vulnerability she felt. Her face flamed, sweat trickling from her hair into the collar of her blouse, and she could do nothing but tear the paper umbrella into shreds with trembling fingers.

That was it. An eight-year secret uttered for the first time. It sounded trivial and stupid out loud as though all of that inner turmoil had been for nothing.

Levi remained silent, stunned, and Anna knew she couldn't leave it there, couldn't let those be the last words between them. She sucked in a breath and with shaky, cracked words, continued.

"I know people cheat all the time. I know that. It's in every show and book and film. But she wouldn't tell my dad and she wouldn't let me tell him either. I tried to live with it, forget it, that entire summer before university started... but I couldn't. It made me feel sick, Levi, and I didn't know what my dad would do if he found out. I didn't want to be the one to hurt him with the truth. I shouldn't have *had* to be. So, I left. And I hated her for it. I hated her for ruining my home, my relationship with my dad, with her lies. Every time I looked at her, I saw it. And when Stevie dropped out and came home, I knew I'd have to choose. Go back to the secrets and the lies every time I came home to see her, or do what I always wanted to and stay away for good."

Levi cleared their throat, fingers lacing with hers again. Sympathy riddled their features, and it left Anna's stomach aching. "Stevie doesn't know."

It wasn't a question, but Anna answered it anyway. "No."

"You could have told her. She would have understood."

"I didn't *want* to tell her," Anna admitted. "She was such an idealist. She argued with every cynical comment I ever made, and her parents were always so loved up. She wouldn't have understood."

They softened, squeezed her hand, then looked at her again as though they were waiting for her to cry or scream or walk away. She didn't; instead Anna fixed her focus on the Jack Daniel's whiskey bottle label behind the bar.

"Did Stevie tell you why *she* came home?"

"No. I mean, she got a little distant at uni, so I just assumed she didn't want to do the course anymore. Her heart was always in creative stuff."

"You need to talk to her," Levi said. "And maybe take a few lessons in communication."

Anna's unsettled stomach somersaulted at that, and not in a pleasant way. What was she missing? What did Levi know?

What does it matter? another voice countered, one she had learned to listen to over the years. One that had told her to leave Castell Bay and never come back. She had ignored it only once, when she did decide to return. For the job, she liked to tell herself, and not because the loneliness she'd felt in Cardiff had become too stifling.

"It's ancient history." An echo of Stevie's words, sounding hollow even to Anna's ears. But she couldn't sit here and keep rehashing the past. Something this broken could not be fixed. And Anna hadn't come here to fix anything, even if it was possible to. "There's nothing left to talk about."

She'd loved Stevie once, but Anna had made the decision to end it. She had to live with that.

So, Anna pushed off the bar and made the excuse of an oncoming migraine before Levi could try to speak any more sense into her.

Before she could crumble beneath the beliefs she'd worked hard to uphold all these years.

Before she saw Stevie again and wondered if she'd made a mistake.

Four

Anna dared to venture to Castell Bay's weekly market the following morning if only to get out of the stuffy, empty apartment for a few hours — and to escape the ear-splitting, endless screams of children enjoying a bank holiday weekend on the beach.

Nothing had changed since she'd left eight years ago. Arnold still manned the fruit and veg stall with his prize-winning cabbages; Paddy still offered tasters of his renowned meat and potato pies to every passerby regardless of the fact that everyone in the village must, at some point, have already tried them before; and Marigold had taken over in her mother's stead selling souvenirs, clotted cream fudge, and hard-boiled sweets.

But in the far corner beside Archie's Ice Cream, the handmade jewellery stand where she had bought her first — and only — belly button ring no longer stood. It had been replaced by the Little Shop of Driftwood. Behind the table of seashell decorations and wood carvings, Stevie chatted with her customers, wearing a soft smile while the sun's rays wreathed her in the same buttery shade of gold as her hair.

She lifted her gaze from the short old lady she was assisting, and Anna looked away quickly, wandering across the cobbles to Carrie's stall of vegan candles. It was an effort not to turn back; look over her shoulder; get a second glance at the woman she'd once loved. A deep, traitorous part of her, rooted low in her stomach, her soul, still knew to spark at the sight of Stevie, as though the distance and the radio silence hadn't been enough to snuff out the flames completely; hadn't been enough to forget that unwavering attraction. As though it had been seared permanently, unbreakably into Anna's muscle memory: seeing her and just... loving.

But Anna couldn't go back to that. She'd ruined it long ago, and Stevie deserved better. Maybe she already had it. She hadn't found it in her to ask Levi if she was seeing anyone.

To distract herself, she picked up a blueberry pie-scented candle and sniffed. She caught the blueberries but not the pie. The scent was nice enough to rid her apartment of the strange, tomato soup-ish smell the previous tenants had left behind.

"Oh my goodness!" The exclamation pierced through the muffled conversation of shoppers; its source, Carrie, who had slapped her hands to her cheeks and as a result, looked a little bit like the ghostly figure in Munch's *Scream* painting. "Anna Conway!"

Anna winced at the attention the dramatics

earned her, and cast Carrie a sheepish wave. The woman was an old neighbour and had probably seen Anna run around the garden in her birthday suit as a toddler more times than either of them would like to count.

"Hello, Carrie," Anna smiled.

"Is that it? 'Hello, Carrie'?" Carrie's voice rose even higher in pitch, until she was certain the Golden Retriever tied up to the next stall over would have to translate. "I haven't seen you in eight years, you little madam. Where have you been?"

"Cardiff. I should have kept in touch, I know, but...."

"Does your mother know you're back? I saw her only yesterday and she didn't mention a thing! I'll be having words."

"Actually, Carrie, she doesn't. I...." Anna sucked in a sharp breath, nerves jostling at the thought of her mother finding out — and Jen *would* find out now. Even without her foghorn voice, Carrie loved gossip. "I haven't spoken to her yet."

Carrie's spider leg-thin eyebrows furrowed. "But whyever not?"

Anna didn't have time to answer. A woman beside her did it for her, her arm brushing Anna's as she pushed through the small queue of customers. "I happen to be wondering the same thing, Carrie."

An ever-present knot tightened in Anna's stomach at the sound of the familiar, clipped voice so much like her own. With a gulp, she turned just enough to confirm her fears, and then immediately wished she hadn't.

Jen Conway stood as erect as an army sergeant, her fine, silver-streaked hair straightened severely and her hands clasped in front of her. Her lips were pressed into a thin, flat line, grey eyes cold as ice. Anna had not expected a warm welcome, but she had forgotten just how cutting her mother's wrath could be, even when no words were said. Like plunging headfirst into the sea in the middle of winter.

But Anna refused to shrink away as she might have once. She was an adult now and had known what she would be facing coming home. Anna would take it on the chin as she did everything else. So, she regarded her mother just as coolly, unsurprised that Jen would need to wear a coat on a sunny, August day.

"I was going to call," Anna lied finally, because false greetings or even a normal 'hello' felt foreign and unnatural.

"Considering my phone hasn't rung once in eight years, I doubt that very much."

Anna's eyes darted around her. People were watching. People could hear. Carrie included. She placed down the candle and shot Carrie an apologetic smile before escaping the crowd. Her mother followed, heels clicking against stone.

Other than a few more wrinkles and the pale, grey roots of her hair, Jen looked no different.

No warmer. No kinder. No more mother-ish. As a child, Anna had joined all sorts of clubs — gymnastics, sailing, quiz teams — to try to ease those harsh features. She had been at the top of every class, had never once caused an ounce of trouble, had always put in more work than her friends. None of it had worked. There would always be a rift between them, and Jen would always look at Anna as though she was a piece of lint sullying her well-ironed clothes.

"I'm sorry," Anna said, though she wasn't. "You're right. I should have reached out."

But the phone worked both ways. Anna had rarely heard from Jen either.

"Imagine how it must feel, Anna," Jen sniffed. "Seeing your daughter back in town, talking to your friends after not hearing so much as a peep for eight years. Wait until I tell your father."

The smell of fried onions and fatty bacon from the food truck across the way was beginning to make Anna feel sick, and it wasn't the only thing. The thought of her father, of facing him while knowing what she knew, did not help. It only surprised her a little that her parents were still together at all. Then again, Jen was good at burying her secrets.

Your father can never know.

She still heard those words, hissed out like a threat, her mother's fingers clenched around Anna's wrist.

And he didn't. He wouldn't. Because Anna

was too weak. Because Anna didn't want to have to be the one to hurt him.

"I don't know what to say," Anna admitted meekly. "I've been busy."

"Too busy to keep in contact with your family?"

"I needed space."

Jen brushed her hair off her shoulder, scoffing. "Well, you certainly got that. Eight years, Anna."

"You didn't call me either."

"You wouldn't have picked up if I did."

True enough. Anna had expected her to at least try, though. Every birthday, Christmas, and New Year her mother hadn't called felt like a punch in the gut. A reminder of why she'd left, and why she couldn't come back.

Only she was back now. And nothing had changed. Under these circumstances, most mothers would have pulled their daughter into their arms and crooned about how much they'd missed her, regardless of the tension between them.

"Well?" Jen huffed when Anna could not find a decent enough reply. "Is that it? Are you not going to tell me where you're living or why you're back?"

Anna didn't want to tell her mother any of that, but beneath Jen's glare, she was a teenager again, squirming and sweating and trapped. Everything she did was wrong. Every mistake made was her fault.

"I'm living in an apartment by the seafront above the driftwood shop. I got a job offer working for the council here, and I couldn't turn it down."

Jen gave a terse nod. No congratulations. No show of pride. Only a flat, "Right. And are you going to invite your parents around to see it, or is that too much to ask of you?"

The thought of her mother wandering around her small, unimpressive flat, criticising each speck of dust and slightly wonky frame hanging on the wall made her shudder. And seeing her father... How would Anna be able to look him in the eye?

"Well, I haven't had time to unpack or settle in yet. A few weeks from now, perhaps...."

"Good." Jen unbuckled her purse and pulled out a black, leather-bound diary and pen. She licked her finger and flicked through the pages, stopping at a blank one. Anna caught the date in the corner. Three weeks from now exactly. "How's September 3rd? A Friday evening?"

Her mother was nothing if not efficient. Anna forced a taught smile and nodded. "Fine."

"Good. *Oh* —!" her attention slid to something behind Anna, fingers wafting with a queenly wave, "Stevie!"

She nudged past Anna without a second glance, strolling toward Stevie's stall with new-found determination. Anna shifted uncomfortably on her heels for a moment, trying not to notice that she owned the same pleated trousers and pumps her mother currently wore, or else something very similar. Had she unknowingly turned into her? She could be a little bit snobby sometimes. For instance, she didn't like barbecues, would much prefer a decent platter at her favourite tapas bar, and the only pillows she could allow near her bed were duck feather stuffed from John Lewis — to prevent an allergic reaction, of course.

Maybe unknowingly, she had followed in her mother's footsteps. Maybe she was set in her ways, too, and liked to show as much with her outward appearance.

But Anna would never do what Jen had. Anna would never mar a twenty-year marriage with unfaithfulness. And if she ever had children, she would never make them work as hard as she had for a sliver of maternal attention. Never.

They might wear the same trousers, but they didn't have the same hearts.

Anna didn't know what to do when she saw Stevie locked in conversation with Jen. Instinct drove her forward if only to save Stevie from her mother's hostility. As she approached, though, she found Jen scouring the goods laid out on Stevie's stall.

"It's my coworkers birthday next week, and I know she likes your things," Jen was saying. "What do you think?"

"Well," Stevie replied, eyes falling across Anna for just a second before dipping back to the table, "I can personalise a plaque or —"

"Oh, no, nothing that fancy," dismissed Jen. "Just a little keepsake will do."

"I have these seashell necklaces. Or wind chimes." Stevie disrupted the strings of bells, shells, and sea glass, leaving them tinkling as they dangled in her hands. They were lovely, Anna supposed. One of a kind. She tried not to think about the fact that Stevie would not be able to make them anymore — not with shells from Castell Bay, anyway.

"I'll take them." Jen settled, thrusting a twenty-pound note into Stevie's palm without preamble. "I suppose the two of you have already reunited."

"Well…" Stevie worried ,at her lip as she wrapped up the tinkling wind chimes, glancing warily at Anna again. "Anna is living above my shop. It's difficult not to run into her every now and again."

God knew Anna had tried.

"It seems I'm the last to hear of my daughter's return, then."

"Mum," Anna sighed. "Stevie doesn't need to be dragged into this."

With rosy cheeks, Stevie handed the gift bag to Jen. "How's your husband, Mrs. Conway? Still golfing?"

"Never stops." Jen rolled her eyes, though the question seemed to soften her slightly. "I have to pry the club from his hands at bedtime, otherwise he'd sleep with the bloody thing."

Anna frowned. She didn't even know her father had started golfing. How did Stevie?

"Well, it's good to have hobbies." Stevie smiled, though it seemed to be directed at Anna rather than Jen. As though reassuring her. As though Anna knew she was in the middle of something she wished to get out of. It left Anna feeling warm and... irritated. Because after all these years, Stevie still knew her too well, and she could still save Anna from the awkward conversations with her mother. Back then, she'd called herself their buffer. Jen was polite, civil, perhaps even nice, with Stevie, so Stevie always made sure to be there for family dinners, holding Anna's hand beneath the table. Anna would cling onto the limb as though it was her life support.

She shook herself out of the memory, glad when Jen said her good-byes and directed a haughty glower in Anna's direction. "Thank you, Stevie. And Anna, I'll see you on September 3rd."

"You will," Anna muttered, a sigh of relief heaving from her when Jen finally wandered away. "Sorry about that."

Stevie's hazel eyes — more green than brown in the sunlight — assessed Anna carefully, mouth puckered as she chewed on the inside of her cheek. "It's fine."

Whatever friendliness she'd had for Jen dwindled now. Anna should have left then, but her feet wouldn't move. Instead, her eyes danced over the handmade goods on the table, laid out carefully. Wood carvings, wall hangings, necklaces... and bracelets. Anna still had one of those bracelets somewhere, gifted by Stevie for her nineteenth birthday; the last one they'd celebrated together before it all came crashing down. She never wore it, but she couldn't bring herself to throw it away either.

"Look...." Anna began with no real clue as to what would come next, but she didn't need to figure it out. Marigold, the woman who owned the souvenir shop, had strode over with a breakfast muffin from the food truck in either hand and a sparkling grin on her face.

"Hungry, love?" she greeted amiably, handing one of the muffins over.

Stevie took it gratefully. "You're a star."

"Well, it wasn't completely selfless. I was hoping to put in another order. The tourists love your lighthouses and wall hangings."

Anna stepped back from the conversation, unsure if it would be rude to walk away completely without saying good-bye. The conversation wasn't finished. But what else was she going to say?

"Well... " Stevie glanced hesitantly at Anna, "I'm not sure how many I can do this time. With the new bylaws, I'll have to travel to Aberystwyth to get more materials, and I don't know how much I'll be able to find."

Great. Anna was still the villain of the village, ruining businesses, destroying the sales of

Stevie's beloved handmade creations.

"Right…" Marigold glanced between them as though trying to gauge the atmosphere. "Okay. Well, I'll pay you extra for the travel costs. I'm running low on stock, though, so if you could make thirty lighthouses and sixty wall hangings for three or four weeks' time…."

"*Sixty*?" Stevie's eyes bulged in surprise. "I don't know, Marigold. Like I said, everything's a bit up in the air at the moment. Even if I had the supplies, it's a big order."

"Oh, Stevie, you've done it before." Marigold slapped Stevie's shoulder as though she was just being silly. "I'll pay you in advance. You needn't worry about that."

"I'm not worrying —"

"Sorry, lovie, stall's getting busy again. Send me the invoice!" Marigold was already wandering away with her muffin still wrapped in her hand, sending a casual wave Stevie's way.

Stevie's eyes fluttered closed as she sucked in a deep breath, pinching the bridge of her nose. It left Anna swimming in guilt she didn't want to feel. Guilt she shouldn't have to feel. She was protecting the coast with her bylaws. She hadn't *meant* to cause problems for Stevie in the process.

"Stevie," Anna began again, weakly.

But when Stevie lifted her gaze, she wasn't looking at Anna. "Excuse me."

Apparently, she wasn't worried about abandoning the stall, because that was what she did.

Anna watched her go, half-wondering if it was her fault, if she had upset her ex, but Stevie didn't stop too far away, and when she did, she fell into the arms of a very frail version of Jack Turner.

Anna's heart stuttered at the sight of him, thin and wispy-haired and unsteady on his feet. A ghost of the witty, good-natured man Anna remembered him being. Barely recognisable at all, hunched over a walking stick with his wife, Bryn, on his arm.

He didn't look well. He didn't look like himself at all.

And Anna wondered if she might have missed something vital in those eight years away from Castell Bay, because when Stevie pulled away, keeping a hand locked in Jack's, she looked just about ready to cry.

Anna didn't feel too far off herself.

Stevie couldn't sleep, and at about three-thirty a.m., she stopped trying. Instead, she rose with the singing birds, before the sun showed even a glimpse of itself on the horizon, and walked down to the beach without so much as brushing her hair.

The pebbles grinding beneath her feet sounded too loud so early. The tide had dragged backwards, its faint, grey waves whispering with the mild wind in the distance. It was becoming a habit, coming down here before the rest of the world woke, especially in summer when the tourists would spill in with their excited, noisy families in a few hours. It was the only peace she ever got — but this morning, her mind would not even grant her that small gift.

She was worrying again. Worrying about the enormous order Marigold had put in at the market yesterday and her father, who had not been able to remember her name last night, and the fact that if she could not find another beach to gather her materials, she would lose the shop, and then the house, and then who would care for Jack? With him so sick, her mother didn't have time to work, instead spending her days caring for a husband who was gradually slipping away.

They relied on Stevie, even if they didn't say so.

Stevie toed a branch of driftwood sourly. It was big enough to make at least two carvings with, if not three. And over there, sea glass was scattered and sun-bleached shells lay untouched.

It was still dark. The beach was empty. Nobody would see her if she took them. Nobody would know.

Eyes narrowed with determination, she walked home to get a basket and spare canvas bag for the large piece of driftwood and then slipped out again. Stuff the fines. Stuff Anna and her stupid little laws. Nobody would be able to prove that she had scoured the beach before dawn.

And nobody did. Not the next day, or the day after, or the day after that. Even with Anna's apartment window overlooking the beach, she never got caught.

So she carried on with her secret driftwood heists, no matter how exhausting it was waking up so early. And she began to find a thrill in it all.

Five

Stevie was quite startled when Levi and the twins burst through the shop door at the very same time that Anna appeared from the back entrance behind her.

Since Anna and Stevie were still very much avoiding one another at all costs, the latter was the strangest part of it, so she put off facing it and turned her attention to Lois and Ralph first, giving them a tight, Auntie Stevie hug that they inevitably tried to wiggle out of.

"Did you bring me ice cream today?"

"Nope!" Ralph and Lois chorused at the same time as Stevie straightened again. She tried not to notice that Anna still stood behind her. Maybe she was about to enforce a new law: no hugging children, perhaps, or no feeding the gulls chips out on the seafront. Either way, her presence cast a dark shadow through the store.

"I'm beginning to think you like them more than me," Levi said, hands suspiciously full with the twin's matching green backpacks. Stevie knew too well what those meant. Her evening had just been filled. "Anyway, is it alright if I leave them with you two for a bit? The thing is, I have a dentist appointment and Quentin is working late to-night."

"Wait," Stevie glanced between Levi and Anna and then the twins, panic seizing her as Levi handed her the backpacks. "What?"

"I'll only be a couple of hours!" They were already sauntering away towards the door.

"What dentist appointment takes a couple of *hours*?" Anna asked, and for once, Stevie was inclined to agree.

"Well, I'm having a really deep clean. Gums and all. But don't worry, with two of you, they'll be no problem at all!" they called with a wave. "Bye! Thank you! See you soon, monkeys!"

"*Levi*!" Stevie shouted desperately, but it was too late. The door fell shut, Levi gone, and two five-year-olds were sticking their hands in a box of the postcards Stevie bought from Marigold.

She whipped around defensively, crossing her arms over her chest. "Did you know about this?"

Anna lifted her hands in surrender. "*No*. Levi told me to meet them down here so we could take the kids for ice cream."

And Stevie doubted it was a coincidence that afterwards, they just so happened to remember that they had a two-hour dentist appointment that couldn't wait on the very same day Quentin worked late.

"They planned this on purpose," Stevie groaned, and then: "Lois, don't touch that mirror!"

Lois blinked and ran towards the dollhouse instead of the shell-framed mirrors that, in hindsight, should have probably been put somewhere out of reach of clumsy children. Ralph was quite happy to continue sifting through the postcards, managing to crease every single one of them.

"Why?"

"Remember when we had that little fight on the pier when we were dating?" Stevie asked. "I wouldn't talk to you because you dream-cheated on me with Anne Hathaway and I thought that meant you didn't love me anymore."

Anna rolled her eyes. "How could I forget?"

"And then Levi locked us in that rusty chicken coop behind their house and wouldn't let us out until we made up."

"Yeah?" she asked. "And?"

Stevie motioned to the twins as though it was obvious. "They're chicken-cooping us again."

Realisation dawned across Anna's features, and then she grimaced. "Ugh. That slimy b — " she clamped down the curse and went for, "*barnacle*. How could they use their kids to manipulate us?"

Stevie scoffed in agreement, though she had to admit, it was clever and very typical of her best friend. "At least this time it doesn't involve being trapped in a confined space. I was convinced I'd caught bird flu for months after."

Anna scraped her dark hair back, her hip pressed against the counter. Stevie could practically hear the cogs whirring in her brain as she glanced between the twins. "So, what do we do? I'll take one and you take the other?"

A good idea, except the twins had never been separated a day in their lives. They were even in the same nursery class. Stevie wasn't going to be the one to inflict their first experience of separation anxiety upon them.

"Auntie Stevie, can we go to the fair?" Lois asked before Stevie could say so, pointing to the window. Pink and blue lights danced with the low evening sun across the beach — they'd been blinding Stevie from where she worked all week. And the screams from kids reeling around the waltzers had given her a constant headache each time she opened a window.

But it was better than being stuck here full of breakable goods, she supposed. Trying to find a way to co-parent with Anna wouldn't be easy.

She turned to Anna now expectantly. "Are you coming?"

"To the *fair*?" Anna repeated as though Stevie was actually asking her to hop on a plane to Australia rather than embark on a ten-minute walk down the beach.

"It will keep them busy." Stevie shrugged, already gathering the twins' backpacks and making sure she had her purse with her. "We can get them all wired up on sugar so they run Levi ragged later."

The corner of Anna's mouth twitched with the beginnings of a smile. "I forgot how cunning you can be."

If the kids weren't there, Stevie might have shut down at the mention of their past, doing all she could to bat Anna and the memories away. As it were, sliding backpacks onto two tiny pairs of shoulders, Stevie only waggled her eyebrows.

"Payback's a b —" She clamped down the swear word before the twins heard it, instead settling on: "A beach. Payback's a beach."

Anna had found out long ago that, much like her mother, she did not have a maternal bone in her body, and looking after the twins only proved it. It was Stevie who knew what to do with them when they reached the fair on the pier; Stevie who guided Ralph's fishing pole with him while they played hook a duck, winning him a Scooby-Doo plush toy; Stevie who held Lois's hands when she started to get scared in the funhouse. Anna felt useless, a spectator, the only thing she could contribute was candy floss that had dyed the children's mouths and hands pink and blue.

It didn't help that spending time with Stevie was uncomfortable, and both of them were making a conscious effort not to make too much eye contact or stand too close in the attraction queues. Their mission of sugaring up the kids was at least working — perhaps a little too well, since Ralph was currently spinning around and laughing maniacally while they decided what to do next.

With the sun inching towards the horizon, Anna shivered against the brisk wind blowing in from the sea. She seemed to be the only one who felt it in all the excitement. Even Stevie's eyes danced like a child's against the flashing lights of the Jump and Smile ride, its hurtling benches filled with screaming people. Anna wanted to vomit just watching it.

"Alright, kids. What's next?" asked Stevie. "Hall of mirrors?"

"*Boring*!" Lois's shout was earsplitting enough that Anna winced.

"Hmm." Stevie tapped her chin, glancing around the packed pier. Anna did the same. The twins were too young for many of the rides, thank goodness — Anna could not have managed the small roller coaster hanging over the water's edge or the swing ride that went taller than the Ferris wheel. "Bouncy castle?"

"*No*! That's rubbish!" Ralph bellowed, stumbling out of his ungraceful pirouettes looking slightly pale. The teacups weren't an option, either, unless Anna wanted to end up covered in vomit.

"What about the dodgems?" Anna suggested as the sound of bumper cars clattering together caught her attention. "I can take one and you can take the other."

"Alright, if you're paying." Stevie's roguish grin left Anna's breath jammed in her throat. She didn't think she'd seen Stevie smile, *really* smile, since she'd been back, especially not for her. Anna had forgotten how bright and all-consuming it was, all gapped teeth and swollen cheeks. "Who wants to drive with me?"

Both children thrust their hands up, shouting, "I do! Me!"

Stevie's nose wrinkled in amusement. "You can't *both* drive with me! Who wants to drive with Auntie Anna?"

Their eagerness dwindled quickly, and they both shuffled towards Stevie as though Anna was a child-snatcher trying to lure them away from their parents with lollipops. Anna tried not to take it personally. She tried to force a smile. But it wasn't easy. She would never be as close to them as Stevie was. Maybe it was her fault, but she had a feeling that even if she hadn't been away for most of their life, they'd still prefer Stevie.

Stevie huffed, leading Ralph towards Anna. Anna reached her hand out and then regretted it when Ralph's clammy, sticky fingers curled around hers.

"Ralph, you can go with Anna." Stevie bent down to whisper not very quietly in his ear: "She's a better driver than me, anyway, so you'll win."

That seemed to cheer him up, and the children set off skipping toward the dodgems. Anna and Stevie wandered behind, Anna swallowing down her unease as she got out her purse.

"Don't take it personally," Stevie said. "They

just don't know you yet. With their upbringing, they're still hesitant around new people sometimes."

"I'm no good with kids anyway." Anna shrugged as nonchalantly as she could. "Not like you are."

"I've had more practice." It didn't sound like a snipe, but it felt like one.

Shivering, Stevie tucked her hands around her waist, her floral skirt rippling around her legs and her hair windswept. But still beautiful. Still so familiar. When they were younger, she and Anna would make out at the top of the Ferris wheel or hold hands as they rode the ghost train together. Those memories felt closer, easier to touch, standing here. They felt as though they still belonged to Anna where, before, she hadn't wanted to claim them. The attractions and layout and even the hot dog van were identical to the ones she remembered. Nothing had changed.

Nothing but them.

Without meaning to, Anna's eyes slipped from Stevie's eyes to her pink, salt-dried lips. They were still the same too. Maybe even a little plumper.

No. Ancient history. Anna couldn't have those feelings anymore.

She tore her gaze away and tried to remember what they'd been talking about. The kids, who had already gotten in line for the dodgems. Anna's lack of experience.

"Any tips?"

"If all else fails, bribe them with chocolate and ice cream," Stevie said. "Not to compare them to animals, but they're a bit like dogs. Not as cute, but if you bring them enough treats, they'll learn to love you."

Anna snorted ungracefully and then pressed her hand to her mouth. "Right. Got it. Thanks."

Stevie stopped, lips parting as though she was going to say something else. But Anna never found out what it was. Instead, Stevie wandered toward the twins without a glance back to see if Anna followed.

And for a moment, Anna could only stand and breathe in the citrus perfume Stevie left behind and wonder how she could have left her so easily back then.

There was so much of Stevie to miss — Anna only truly realised that now, when she was wrapped in her presence again, with a desperate part of her always reaching out for something she couldn't have.

There was something between them still. Anna felt it.

∞∞∞

In the end, Anna and Ralph *were* better on the driving front, just as Stevie had predicted. She and Lois had still given it their best shot, zooming around the arena in their bumper car while Anna and Ralph tailed them. They had just hit the edges and other people once or twice.

Or thirteen times.

When they stepped back onto the pier, Stevie realised that her cheeks and throat ached from so much laughing. She couldn't remember the last time she'd had so much fun. Lois had loved every moment of steering the wheel and pretending to honk at oncoming traffic.

However, her plot to deliver the twins back to Levi hyped up on sugar seemed to have the opposite outcome. They chose to take their final ride on the carousel, Stevie perched on a white unicorn with a sleepy Ralph, and Anna on the brown horse beside her with Lois. One hand clung to the pole and the other to Ralph, keeping him close to her chest as the tinkling music lulled in time with the rises and falls of the horses and carriages.

"They're eerily quiet," Anna observed, the wind sifting through her dark hair as she craned her neck to make sure Lois was still breathing. She was a little more alert than her brother, at least, whose eyes were already fluttering closed.

"We've tired them out." Stevie couldn't help but smile softly, feeling warm and nostalgic and fuzzy beneath the golden lights of the carousel, with Ralph cosying up to her as though she was the safest place in the world. Being an aunt was the most special thing in her universe. "I think they had fun."

"I did too," Anna admitted. "Though I didn't know horses and unicorns were friends." She motioned to each of their steeds in turn.

Indeed, they had ventured into a land of mixed species. Biting back a laugh, Stevie dared a glimpse at Anna. Her cheeks were rosy, grey eyes gleaming and hair knotted. Alive. Here with Stevie, somehow.

"Don't tell Levi you enjoyed yourself," Stevie warned, unwilling to admit she felt the same. "They don't need more incentive to meddle again."

"Right." Anna laughed softly as the ride slowed to a stop. She and Lois hopped off their horse, but on the saddle of Stevie's unicorn, Ralph didn't move an inch. She peered over his dark head of curls to find that he was fast asleep, faint snores drifting from his gaping mouth.

Stevie couldn't help but soften, running a delicate finger over his silken cheek to see if he would stir. He didn't.

"Dead to the world," Anna whispered. "Should we wake him?"

"No. I'll carry him." It was only a ten-minute walk across the beach, and Ralph was light enough. Dragging an exhausted five-year-old home would be no fun. "Can you hold onto him while I get down?"

Anna did, a hand at his back to keep him steady until Stevie had dismounted and was prepared to pick him up. She expected him to wake again when she lifted him beneath his arms and tucked him close to her chest, but his heavy head rested on her shoulder and stayed there without complaint.

Lois, apparently, still had energy to burn. When they left the pier, she ran ahead of them across the beach, chasing seagulls and drawing wobbly shapes in the sand. It was rare she got to have fun without her brother. It must have been freeing to find herself able to.

Anna carried her jelly sandals, staying at Stevie's side. A smile crossed her lips each time she looked at Ralph sleeping in Stevie's arms, and Stevie tried not to blush beneath the attention.

"Do you want kids of your own?" Anna's question was barely audible above the waves splashing onto the sand.

Stevie shrugged, forgetting that the motion might disturb Ralph. But she didn't think even a helicopter landing on the beach could drag him from his peaceful slumber now, because the rhythm of his snores stayed the same. "No. I don't think so."

She might have in another life. There was something maternal in her, that intrinsic need to nurture, but she had spent so long relying on it to care for her father that if she ever got the chance to live a life of her own, she'd much rather focus on herself for a while.

Anna's brows lifted as she tucked her hair behind her ear.

"That surprises you," Stevie pointed out. Good. She liked surprising Anna. She liked proving that they no longer knew one another as they once had — as much for her own benefit as Anna's.

"It does. The way you look out for the twins… It's easy to picture you being a mother, that's all. It always was."

Stevie tried to quell the warmth rising in her at that. It wasn't even a compliment, but it somehow felt like one all the same. And Stevie liked that Anna saw her that way. Maybe she would want kids one day. Maybe she would have wanted them with Anna in another life.

If they'd lasted. If Anna hadn't turned out to be about as reliable as those rusted coin machines in the arcade where the pennies always ended up jammed in the slots.

"Do you?" Stevie couldn't help but ask. "Want kids, I mean?"

"Maybe one day," Anna admitted. "It's difficult to imagine. I'm not… I don't know."

Stevie wanted to ask what that meant but couldn't. She couldn't have conversations like this with Anna. She focused her gaze ahead again, where Lois was hunched over, picking up shells. "Does she know that's a one-hundred-pound fine?"

For a moment, she thought that Anna might actually scold Lois. Her spine straightened, mouth parting with phantom words, but eventually, she sighed and shook her head. "I'll let her off this time."

If only the same courtesy was extended to Stevie. It didn't matter in the end. Lois dropped the shells and asked Anna to pick her up too, and she fell asleep in Anna's arms before they reached the shop. They went through the back entrance, rising slowly up the stairs and into Anna's apartment. Anna had offered her bed for the twins until Levi returned.

Nothing had been unpacked yet, other than the necessities: kitchen appliances, a TV, and a stack of instant noodles. Anna led Stevie into the back room, where only a double bed and wardrobe resided. The bed was at least made, and Stevie and Anna lowered the twins onto it carefully. Stevie had to shimmy the duvet out from under them to tuck them in, placing a kiss on each of their foreheads before Anna turned out the light, then Stevie closed the door on the darkness.

It might not have been her plan but it felt like an accomplishment to have left them so peaceful. She forgot for a moment where she was, collapsing onto the sofa as though it was her own and resting her head on the cushion behind her. "Peace and quiet."

"Do you want a cup of tea?"

"Please. A drop of milk and — "

"Two sugars," Anna completed for her. "I remember."

Something in Stevie's chest fluttered, but she refused to pay it any heed. "Thanks."

The boiling kettle at least meant that for a

few minutes, they didn't have to talk. But when Anna sat beside her on the couch, handing her the hot mug, it was an effort for Stevie to do anything but fidget and glance around the room as though something might pop out and tear them away from the static-filled silence.

"I saw your parents at the market on Sunday," Anna said, placing her own cup down and crossing her legs. "How are they?"

Stevie gulped. Shrugged. Lied. "They're okay."

"It's just… your dad. He looked different."

Ill. He looked ill. Because he was. But Stevie didn't want to tell Anna that. She didn't want Anna to feel sympathy or guilt because of it.

After the first stroke, Stevie had been in denial about the seriousness of her father's illness. Dropping out of university was supposed to be temporary, and she hadn't had enough time or energy to tell Anna the truth; hadn't wanted to even admit that truth aloud. Naively, Stevie had expected Jack to get better. He hadn't. And Anna had never come back to her, instead breaking things off before they could talk about it. What was the point in bringing it all up now, when that infinite rift yawned out between them?

"Did he?" Stevie questioned without conviction, tracing the rim of her mug absently.

"Is he unwell?"

A knock at the door saved Stevie from having to answer. She placed the mug down swiftly and answered with a glare when she found Levi standing in the hallway, looking sheepishly smug. "Hello. Did you have fun?"

"You're lucky that there are two sleeping children in the next room," she scolded, stepping aside for them to wander in.

They did, thrusting their hands into their pockets and casting Anna a wave. "*Sleeping*? They never sleep. Did you drug them? Because it's okay with me, but social services look down on things like that, I think."

"We took them to the fair," Anna answered, rising from the couch with a glower. "How are your teeth?"

"My teeth?" Levi frowned.

"The dentist, Levi."

"Oh!" Levi snapped their fingers and then flashed a gummy grin. "Sparkling, see?"

They looked no different than they had before, but Stevie hadn't expected them to. "We don't appreciate being chicken cooped."

"Chicken cooped?"

"You locked us in a chicken coop last time we fought, remember?" Anna reminded.

"*Oh*." Levi nodded in understanding. "Well, it worked, didn't it?"

It had, only because Stevie hadn't wanted to spend the rest of her existence smelling hay and finding feathers stuck to her clothes. "You're not clever and you're not smart, Levi Peters."

Levi smirked, glancing between them. "I

don't know what you mean."

Stevie rolled her eyes. "I'll help you get the kids into the car."

"Oh, before you do," Levi clapped their hands as though a meeting had commenced, "I was wondering who's driving with who for the annual camping trip this year."

"Annual camping trip?" Anna asked. "You still do that?"

It had been a tradition long before the twins were adopted to drive two hours north to Vernon Valley and make camp in the middle of nowhere every summer. Stevie had forgotten all about it this year, too rushed off her feet. And of course, she hadn't considered that Anna would be invited too, though she should have.

She usually loved it, especially now that Levi had a family of their own and it wasn't just the two of them catastrophising about having to potentially fight off bears and wolves in the wild. But with Anna there ....

Tonight had been uncomfortable enough. Stevie didn't need a whole weekend of it.

"I'll have to pass this year, I think. I'm overrun with all the shop stuff, and —"

"Nope." Levi lifted a hand to silence her. "You're coming. You both are. I'll drag you there kicking and screaming if I have to."

"Yeah, as fun as it sounds, I'm not big on camping these days," said Anna, as though she had ever been big on camping to begin with. The one time they'd convinced her to go, just after their final exams, she had tripped over a tree root on a hike and twisted her ankle. They had ended up in Accident and Emergency for most of the trip.

"No!" Levi denied with a shake of their head. "You're both coming. End of discussion. It's the first year the kids will really enjoy it and I want you both there."

Stevie sighed. "Levi —"

"Please." Levi stuck out their lower lip, looking about the same age as Ralph. "You guys are family. It will be fun, promise."

And for all her dread, Stevie couldn't refuse when it came to family. She was grateful just to be accepted into Levi and Quentin's. She huffed, resigned and refusing to look at Anna as she said, "Fine. I'll go."

Anna rolled her eyes and sank into the couch cushions with a groan. "*Fine.*"

When Levi cheered joyously, they both shushed them at the same time.

Six

Anna couldn't sleep. Most likely because after the twins had left, she'd finished off their bag of sugary sweets while binge-watching the *Great British Bake Off*, but the fact she couldn't stop thinking about Stevie and the camping trip didn't help either. It was dangerous, being this close to her again. Levi meant no harm, but that didn't mean their matchmaking games were harmless.

She had enjoyed Stevie's company too much tonight. She had enjoyed pretending that there was not an eight-year rift between them.

After giving up on sleep, she hauled herself out of bed, cracking open a window when she found the living room stuffy and uncomfortable.

And then she stilled.

A silhouette ambled down the beach, something swinging in their hands. Anna checked her watch. It was little past four o'clock in the morning, the first grey wisps of dawn seeping into the night sky. What the hell was someone doing on the beach at this ungodly hour? Was it a runner? A murderer. Whatever they were holding wasn't big enough to be a body… unless they had killed a hamster or a cat.

If the figure didn't stop suddenly and crouch, Anna might have dismissed it and made herself a cup of chamomile tea, but they did, and then they gathered a long branch of driftwood and placed it into what must have been a basket in their hands.

Anna's eyes narrowed. *Crafty bugger.* Somebody clearly thought they'd found a way around Anna's new bylaws, and she'd caught them in the act.

Forgetting that she was in her *Back to the Future*-themed pyjamas, she slipped on her slipper boots and headed out into the night. She felt strange and slightly out of her body wandering around at this time, sand and pebbles crunching beneath her thin slippers and the warm wind seeping through her cotton pyjama bottoms. The moon led her on her way, a bright crescent reflected in fragments across the sea hanging just above the beachcomber's head.

It was only as Anna got closer that she recognised the round figure and short hair. And it didn't surprise her an ounce that Stevie would go out of her way to outsmart Anna. She almost wanted to laugh, in fact, when Anna's footsteps caused Stevie to straighten from the pile of driftwood.

Stevie's eyes were wide, startled, a hand on her chest until she saw who greeted her and groaned. "You must be joking."

Anna eyed the basket of driftwood and

shells in Stevie's hand, an eyebrow raised. "I'm beginning to think that you haven't been following the new bylaws at all, Stevie."

"I don't know what gave you that impression." With a dejected huff, Stevie emptied out her basket, the materials tumbling at her feet. "How did you find me out?"

"Couldn't sleep." Anna smiled wryly, raking back her sleep-tangled hair and hoping she did not look too dishevelled. Stevie didn't. No more than usual, anyway. She wasn't in her pyjamas, either. How often had she been doing this?

"It must have been your spidey senses tingling." It surprised Anna when Stevie collapsed onto the pebbles, legs crossed and eyes staring unseeingly towards the glowing horizon. "I suppose I owe you one-hundred pounds."

Anna rolled her eyes and sat beside her, pulling her knees to her chest. Of course she wouldn't give her a fine. No matter what Stevie believed, she couldn't be that cruel. It didn't mean she would give in so easily either, though. "Are you honestly that desperate for materials?"

"You heard Marigold's order," Stevie grumbled. "It takes a lot of wood to carve my ornaments."

"I'm sure if you asked her for an extension, she'd understand."

In a croaking whisper, Stevie admitted, "I need the money."

"Oh." Anna didn't know what to say to that.

She hadn't realised. The vulnerability cracking in Stevie's voice overwhelmed her with concern, with guilt. "Why? Is everything okay?"

"Running a business is expensive, Anna." Stevie scoffed and stood up with her empty basket, making to leave.

But Anna didn't want her to. She needed more, needed to understand, needed to stop letting them both hide behind half-answers and moments of avoided eye contact. She needed Stevie to look at her in the dawn light, needed...

Her fingers curled around Stevie's wrist, pulling her back gently. Stevie looked down at her, lips parting in surprise, and Anna wondered what she saw. She had every right to hate her, but Anna found nothing bitter in those eyes. Only raw, immeasurable exhaustion — in the dark circles beneath her eyes and the paleness of her face, in the slack way she held herself.

She was battling with something, and Anna didn't know what, hadn't earned the right to know, and that killed her more than anything else between them. Because, once, she would have been the first person Stevie talked to. And now she couldn't be. She never would be again.

"I never meant to hurt you." Anna rose to her feet with her hand still tugging at Stevie's arm, their faces falling inches apart until she could hear Stevie's ragged breaths and see the small cluster of pin-sized freckles peppered beneath her jaw. She didn't know if she meant now, with the bylaws, or before, when she'd ran away and broken them.

"Then why did you?" Stevie's whispered words sounded too much like a plea, and Anna's knees almost fell out from under her in response. They definitely weren't talking about the bylaws.

"I couldn't stay. I couldn't come back."

"Why?"

Anna licked her lips, wondering if Stevie would ever understand. Maybe she had at least deserved the option to try. Maybe Anna had made a mistake in never telling her. She sucked in a breath and said, "My mum. She... She cheated on my dad."

Stevie's brows knitted together, a crease sinking between them. "When?"

"The summer before uni." Anna could have let go of Stevie's arm if she wanted. Her feet were planted firmly in the pebbles. She wasn't going anywhere. But Anna didn't want to let go. The last time she had, she'd felt empty for months.

"Why didn't you tell me?"

"Because... It felt like the biggest thing in my world, and you would have made it small. You liked fixing things. You liked making everything positive and easy, and I loved that about you, but you couldn't fix this, Stevie. Nobody could. And I really didn't want you to try."

It was as simple as Anna could make it. Maybe it wouldn't make sense. Maybe all of this was pointless. But something flickered in Stevie's expression, and she didn't think that was the case. "You mean the way Levi does with us now. Pretending that if they force us together, everything will magically be better and we'll skip into the sunset hand in hand."

"Right." Anna's heart thudded desperately.

Meekly, considering, Stevie muttered, "I didn't know I was like that."

"It was never a bad thing."

Finally, Stevie pulled her wrist away, shifting hesitantly. "And is that why? Because we could have found a way through it if it was. Even if you couldn't tell me, we could have figured something out."

"I know."

"But you never gave it a chance."

"I know." Regret seeped into Anna's words as she agreed.

"I thought it was about me... About us."

"I know. I suppose I lost my way with us. I worried that it wouldn't work with distance between us, and I wanted to save myself the heartbreak later down the line. I wanted a clean break from everything that reminded me of home. And you left too, Stevie. You disappeared without even talking to me about it. What was I supposed to think?"

"I..." A fire seemed to ebb in Stevie's eyes. Her shoulders slumped a moment later as she ran her hand across her drawn face. "I had my own stuff to work out. I didn't think you'd give up on me so quickly." And then, when Anna had no response: "So, you didn't stop loving me?"

The question felt like a sledgehammer breaking through Anna's ribs, her heart. Is that what Stevie thought? Is that what Anna let her think?

"No." Without warning, a tear dribbled down Anna's cheek. She staunched it with her palm quickly. "No, loving you was never the problem, Stevie."

Not then, anyway. Now it was — because she still did, she realised. She still loved Stevie, even as different and closed off as she was. She had seen glimpses of the woman she'd fallen for last night, the one who laughed loudly and unabashedly, the one who cared for everyone around her, the one who Anna had lain awake with at night, content in hours-long silences, fingers dancing across spines and legs entwined.

"And yet you dropped me as though I meant nothing." Stevie swallowed, taking another step back as though Anna was a bonfire and Stevie stood close enough to be burned.

Anna tried not to flinch. "I know. I'm sorry. But it felt like you did the same to me."

Silence. Waves crashing and pooling. Them, breathing so heavily Anna couldn't distinguish which rhythm belonged to her lungs and which to Stevie's. A car passing by on the deserted road.

"Maybe... Maybe we just weren't good for each other, then. Anyway." Stevie sniffed, walls rebuilding themselves before Anna's eyes. Maybe that was their problem. They both liked to pretend they didn't feel, didn't hurt. "Ancient history, right?"

The two words were a blade slicing between them, making Anna recoil. Because the tears in her eyes and the roiling storm in her gut were not ancient history. They were *now*. Her present. Her whole, entire, pathetic life. Anna couldn't rid herself of them no matter how she tried.

"Stevie —"

"My address is still the same. For the fine, I mean."

"Stevie, I'm not going to give you a fine," Anna said — begged.

But she didn't know if Stevie heard, because her ex was already making her way off the beach, away from Anna, and Anna didn't have the strength to stop her. She never did seem to have what it took to get her back.

Seven

No matter how hard she had tried — and God knows she had — Stevie could not get out of Levi's camping trip.

She loved camping. She loved spending quality time with the twins and Levi and Quentin. She loved the escape, the peace and quiet, the simplicity of waking up in the middle of nowhere without worrying about what was for breakfast or whether her father needed help taking a bath or, oh God, had she slept through her alarm? She loved that the smell of fire and earth clung to her until she felt as though she was rooted in the world in a more vital way.

What she didn't love was spending an hour and a half in the car with only her ex-girlfriend for company. No, that part wasn't ideal at all, especially since they had barely spoken since the night on the beach. When the fine didn't come, Stevie had gone back to the beach a few mornings after, if only to test Anna. From the sand, she had seen the curtain twitch in the apartment window, a silhouette shifting and then disappearing, but when Stevie had collected a heap of driftwood and shells and Anna had not emerged in her retro pyjamas to reprimand her, she knew Anna would not stop her again.

She didn't know why that left a small kernel of disappointment in her. Maybe because they still had so much to talk about, so many things left unsaid, and airing it out before dawn on the deserted beach somehow felt easier than in daylight. Maybe because, for all the pain it caused, Stevie wanted to hear Anna tell her again that she hadn't stopped loving her. Maybe because she was still weak when it came to Anna, and perhaps always would be.

Whatever had passed between them on the beach didn't return during their winding journey into the valleys, though. Anna had offered to drive since she had the better car — which wasn't a difficult competition against Stevie's thirty-year-old Volvo — and Stevie sat in the passenger seat, pretending to be mesmerised by the endless, merging trails of trees fringing the road. An old Beatles album Anna had owned back when they were dating drifted quietly from the stereo, and the only time either of them said a word was when Anna encountered a terrible driver and couldn't keep her temper at bay. "Son of a beluga whale!" and, "Get off the road, eejit!" were Stevie's favourite so far.

"Are you hungry?" Stevie asked when Anna had not had an outburst in a while, rooting through her backpack for the packed lunch she'd made this morning. "I made jam sandwiches."

"No thank you. I don't like jam."

"Since when? You used to *love* jam." The

words fell out before Stevie could stop them, and her face flamed in the uncomfortable aftermath. Acknowledging old memories of one another felt like crossing a line somehow, as though those versions of themselves were no longer allowed to exist. "Sorry. I... That's none of my business."

Anna shifted in her seat uncomfortably, lip tucked between her teeth as they veered onto a country lane. The dappled sunlight danced across her face, leaving her eyes to flash in unpredictable bursts of blue, green, and silver. Stevie used to watch it happen unabashedly, infatuated by the way Anna could change so quickly, like a mood stone. Now, she forced her gaze away, fiddling with her nose ring absently.

"Look, I know things are... weird," Anna began quietly, "but I'd like to at least try to be friends with you, maybe. If you'd like. If only for this weekend."

Stevie gulped down a long breath, fingers tapping her thigh to the solemn melody of 'Something'. *Could* exes be friends? She didn't know. She'd only fallen in love once in her life, with Anna.

It *would* be nice if they didn't have to spend this weekend pretending as though they didn't know one another at all, though. For the kids and Levi and Quentin, if not for themselves. Stevie deserved to have fun. They all did. She just hoped they wouldn't wind up stumbling between friendship to something else, something fragile and frightening. She couldn't wear her heart on her sleeve just to get it broken again.

"I'd like that too," Stevie admitted. "Just for the weekend."

Anna smiled, eyes flitting to Stevie for a moment. Stevie tried not to notice the genuine joy beaming from her. "Yeah?"

"Yeah."

Anna blew out a breath of relief. "Good."

Stevie nodded, wondering how to navigate these new, friendly waters. She supposed less stilted conversation would be a start, but she didn't know what to talk about, how to try. "So. How are things with your mum?"

Anna winced, and so did Stevie when she remembered the conversation on the beach. Anna probably didn't want to talk about the stern woman who had driven her away from town with her lies and cheating.

"Sorry. I wasn't—"

"No," Anna said. "It's okay. It's… tense. We didn't really talk while I was away, so it's all a bit awkward. I've been trying to avoid her, but she sort of invited herself over to my apartment for dinner next week."

"Is your dad going?"

"Yeah."

"And he… he still doesn't know?"

Anna shook her head, knuckles whitening on the steering wheel. "No. Not as far as I know. I'm dreading it, to be honest."

Stevie could only imagine. Taking care of

her sick father was difficult, but at least her parents loved one another — most of the time. And they loved her too, even if they forgot to say so these days. She couldn't imagine it being any other way. Then, she remembered evenings spent holding Anna's hand under the kitchen table as her mother chided her about grades and her future, picking her apart piece by piece. Stevie only wanted to hold her together. Afterwards, Anna would spend hours not saying a word, and Stevie had only been able to lie with her and wonder how to make it better. But you couldn't make something like that better. Not when the person who was supposed to love you more than anything only ever found flaws to criticise instead.

With sympathy swelling in Stevie's gut, and that knowledge that Anna had always been grateful for her support, she couldn't help but offer, "I could come if you want. I mean, if it helps."

Anna's brows rose in surprise. "You don't have to. I wouldn't want to subject you to all of my family drama."

"I don't mind." It was true. Stevie only wanted to help. To make sure Anna was okay at the end of the night. Caring about her was a habit she didn't seem to want to break yet.

After a long pause, in which Stevie spent questioning almost everything she had said to Anna in the last five minutes, Anna finally agreed, "Then I'd love that. Thank you."

Stevie only nodded and bit back a smile. "No

problem."

∞∞∞

"Where's your tent, Anna?"

It was Quentin who asked, eyeing Anna's very empty hands while Stevie and Levi got to work on their own. It was a valid question too. One she had only just thought to ask herself. Somehow, it hadn't occurred to her to bring one.

"Do I look like the sort of person to own a tent?"

Levi smirked as they hammered the pegs into the damp earth, sycamore seeds and pine needles caught in their loose curls. "Were you planning on sleeping with us?"

"No," she scoffed, resting her hands on her hips and glaring at an obscenely loud blackbird screeching in the green canopy above their heads.

Anna did not like camping. She did not like being stuck in the middle of nowhere without a phone signal. She did not like that something always ended up going wrong on her end — sprained joints or forgotten belongings or Britain's unpredictable weather. She did not like sleeping on the floor, sweltering in a sleeping bag while hoping a ravenous pack of foxes would not stumble upon her tent.

But she couldn't say any of this in front of the twins without ruining their joy, so she only scowled deeper and wondered where she *would* sleep tonight. The twins' tent was too small. Quentin and Levi would surely want some alone time. That left...

"You could share Stevie's tent," Quentin suggested, triggering a wave of dread in Anna.

Stevie glanced at Anna warily, and Anna couldn't blame her. It was probably not a good idea to sleep in a confined space with one's ex-girlfriend.

"You know, I'll be fine on the floor out here."

Stevie scoffed. "You're not sleeping outside. Look, my tent is roomy enough. We could top and tail."

Anna sighed, though she did not particularly want to sleep in an open space where forest creatures could easily find her either. And top and tailing *was* very platonic and non-weird, wasn't it?

It was. It would have to be. "Okay. Thank you."

"So what *did* you bring?" Levi questioned. "Clothes? Because that jacket looks more expensive than my car, and very soon it might well have dirt and pigeon poo all over it."

Lois and Ralph burst into a fit of laughter at the word 'poop' and then proceeded to run figure eights around the trees screaming, "Pigeon poop! Pigeon poop!"

Anna scowled again and smoothed down her two-hundred-pound Ted Baker jacket. Not quite as expensive as a car, but just as precious to Anna. In hindsight, maybe wearing it to go camping hadn't been a good idea — but she didn't *own* anything else. She'd spent the last eight years working in the city in pencil skirts and frilly blouses, not hiking through Welsh valleys in leggings and muddy boots. "I brought my pillow. And a cardigan. And —"

"A sense of humour?" Stevie finished, though she was smirking. "Help me pitch this tent, will you? I think I've bent one of these pole thingies."

"You two are useless!" Quentin huffed.

"Well, I did better than last year," said Stevie.

"You didn't do it last year," Levi retorted. "*I* did."

"Exactly. At least I tried this time."

Anna perched on a tree stump, listening to the amusing argument. It was difficult, though. She had missed so much. She felt on the edge of it all, a barrier keeping her at bay. They had made so many memories without her and she could blame nobody but herself.

But she was here now, and the children stopped running to drag her down to the lake, which was just visible from where it gleamed beyond the trees. That had to count for something. "Auntie Anna, come and look at our secret lake!"

"Ooh, can I come?" Stevie followed, having given up on the tent. Levi and Quentin had taken over. She cast a wry wave their way.

"Look, Auntie Stevie!" Ralph pointed and

then crouched over a cluster of small, rich-blue flowers. "Flowers!"

"Oh, yes! They're pretty, aren't they?"

Anna had thought Stevie was feigning excitement for Ralph's sake, but when she stood beside him to get a better look, her eyes seemed to brighten as though she was just as new to the world as the children. Anna couldn't help but smile, heart lifting with admiration.

"These are called cornflowers," said Stevie.

"Am I allowed to pick one?" asked Ralph.

"Well, I don't know about that. Auntie Anna is the environmental expert." Stevie glanced at Anna expectantly.

Anna had always been told not to pick flowers, but she couldn't deny Ralph with his round, pleading eyes. "Go on, then. A few wildflowers won't do any harm."

"You know, we can keep these forever if you want," Stevie said, helping Ralph to gather a few.

Lois picked some too, sniffing them and then pulling a face that made Anna suspect something might have urinated on them. "How?" she asked, all moon-eyed with adorable intrigue.

"Well, if we press them between the pages of a book for a day or so, they'll dry out and flatten instead of dying."

It was something Anna remembered Stevie spending hours on when they were younger. She would pick a flower wherever they went — a buttercup in the sand dunes, a bluebell in the grass

— until her books were full of pressed flowers, the ink smudged and unreadable. She sometimes thought it was the only reason Stevie kept books at all. It felt special that she could pass the tradition down to Lois and Ralph now; offering pieces of herself to them. They weren't just being raised by Levi and Quentin, but by her too.

"Can we do that now?" Ralph asked.

"Well," Stevie checked her pockets comically, "I don't have a book. Do you?"

They shook their heads, pouting.

Anna did. A tattered copy of *Persuasion* that an old coworker had loaned her, never to be read, sat in the glove compartment of her car. "Then it's your lucky day, because I do! It's in my car."

They cheered excitedly and ran back to the campsite, urging Anna to: "Hurry up! Hurry, Auntie Anna!"

Anna chuckled and sprinted back to her car, Stevie lagging behind. Levi and Quentin had almost finished putting up the three tents and seemed happy enough that the kids were being kept entertained. Anna dipped into her car seat and pulled out the book quickly before locking it again, and then passed the book to Stevie to demonstrate.

"You don't mind if the pages smudge?" Stevie asked cautiously.

"Nah," Anna said. "I don't read much anymore. It's fine."

"Okay. Shall we do one each?"

The twins nodded. Crouching so that they could see, Stevie placed the first cornflower between the book's pages. She flicked to a new page next to let Ralph, and then Lois, do the same. And then she closed the book.

"We have to leave them there for a while now and put something heavy on top. How about this log?"

Anna shuddered when Stevie lifted the log up. It was infested with woodlice and worms underneath.

"Creepy crawlies!" Ralph screamed.

"On second thought..." Stevie put the log down and collected a set of stones instead, "These'll do. We'll check again later to see if it's working."

They did, just before settling down for dinner — sausage and beans from a tin which left Anna feeling queasy — in front of a campfire that only Quentin had the skill to start with sticks and stones and a match hidden in his pocket that everyone pretended not to see. Indeed, the cornflowers had flattened into the printed words of Jane Austen, though they hadn't dried properly yet.

"See?" Stevie said, wearing a proud smile. "We can keep these forever, like a memory we can touch."

The twins were awestruck. Anna wasn't — not by the flowers, anyway. But the way Stevie's voice softened when she spoke to the twins, the way she taught them little things no one else would. It was special. Anna felt lucky to witness it. She wished she had that skill. Wished she was half the person Stevie was. And when Stevie pulled out two flattened flowers, leaving the third pressed in the book before handing it back to Anna, tears almost sprang to Anna's eyes.

She wanted to keep this memory, too. And Stevie had let her.

Eight

As much as Stevie loved spending time with the twins, she was glad for the peace when it reached their bedtime. A stifling humidity had blanketed the woods over the afternoon, and even as the sun set, it was everywhere: unavoidable and clinging to her like a second layer of skin.

"Remind me why we need a fire again," she groaned as Levi and Quentin settled behind the flames opposite, cheeks rosy and a sheen of sweat caking their foreheads. Anna sat in a collapsible camp chair adjacent, quiet and unreachable. Stevie didn't know why, and that bothered her.

"For s'mores!" Levi produced a bag of marshmallows from their backpack and rattled them eagerly.

Her sweet tooth must have been malfunctioning because the thought of feasting on roasted marshmallows on top of the awful tinned dinner they'd eaten made Stevie want to throw up. She swiped her sweaty bangs from her face and rose, seeking reprieve from the unnecessary fire. Not that it was any cooler away from it.

"I'll pass. Anyone for a swim instead?" The quaint lake was the only thing for miles where

Stevie might be able to cool down, and they often ended up swimming in it on days like this, the kids splashing about in inflatable armbands and screaming when their feet touched something slimy. Stevie always ended up going home stinking of a stagnant, algae-infested fishpond, but she'd take that over stale body odour any day.

"You should go, Anna," Levi suggested, wiggling their eyebrows. "It's fun."

Anna glanced at them warily. "Is it clean?"

"It's *fun*." Levi sighed, shooing her away. "Go on. It'll be getting dark in a bit, and Stevie might get lost on her own."

A lie. Stevie knew the campsite trails as well as she knew Castell Bay by now. "You're chicken cooping us again."

"I am *not*! Has it ever occurred to you that I might want some alone time with my husband?" Levi laced their fingers through Quentin's pointedly, taking a bite of charred marshmallow.

"Ugh, fine," Anna groused, pushing up from her chair. "I know when I'm not wanted."

Stevie was too sweltering to care either way. She gathered her towels and a fresh set of clothes and wandered down to the lake, not bothering to see if Anna followed. When twigs began to snap behind her, she knew Anna had.

"Should I have gotten a tetanus shot before coming here?" Anna asked as they fell out onto the soggy banks of the lake. The water reflected the mottled purple-grey of the twilit sky, which probably did Anna's hygiene concerns no favours. Even so, it was beautiful. Peaceful. Still. Surrounded by wild shrubbery and leafy, rustling trees.

"You know, I thought I was uptight." Finding a relatively dry patch of grass by the shore, Stevie toed off her boots and socks and then shimmied out of her leggings. It left her in only her sweat-stained tunic, which at least fell to the top of her thighs. She didn't care much for modesty tonight and it was nothing that Anna hadn't already seen.

"I'm not uptight." Anna glowered, and as though to prove it, kicked off her own boots and shucked off her fancy, now dandelion seed-covered jacket. A challenge.

Stevie raised an eyebrow and couldn't help but smirk. She liked this side of Anna, and liked being the only one able to bring it out of her.

With her grey, blazing eyes locked defiantly on Stevie, Anna peeled off her skinny jeans — and didn't stop there. The blouse and vest top came off too, leaving the smooth curves of her freckled belly on show.

It was an effort for Stevie to keep her gaze fixed on Anna's face, to not look down at the more toned, filled out version of a body she had once adored. She had never needed to plunge herself into the lake more, so she turned on her heel and waded into the lake toe by toe, inch by inch, gasping when the surprisingly cool water lapped at her legs, hips, seeping into her underwear and then her tunic. It did nothing to snuff out the heat beginning to uncoil in her stomach, though goose bumps bloomed across her arms all the same.

The water rippled with Anna's presence behind her. Stevie dared turn around, lowering to submerge her shoulders, her arms, the tip of her chin, and almost froze. Anna. In her underwear. The sweat-damp ends of her dark hair curling just above the swell of her breasts.

What were they doing? What had Stevie been thinking?

She hadn't been thinking. She'd been too hot and sticky and uncomfortable to think. She blamed the weather.

But the weather wasn't the problem anymore. It was the storm stirring from her chest to her stomach with the knowledge that if she just reached out, she could run her fingers across Anna's pink, heart-shaped lips.

She swallowed and looked away.

"I bet it's cooler without the shirt." Anna kicked at the water, her head bobbing beneath the surface.

Stevie glanced down at her tunic. It might have been cooler, but she wasn't sure she wanted to take it off. If there was only water and skin between them, it would be too easy to give in. And her body had changed. More than Anna's had. Maybe Anna wouldn't look at her the way she used to, with her stomach rolls and stretch marks. Not that Stevie would have cared if it was the other way around.

Instead of answering, Stevie pinched her nostrils and sank below the surface, lungs burning and feet brushing the grainy silt of the lake's bed. When she rose up, water cascading from the crown of her head and pasting her hair to her temples, she found Anna still watching. Was surprised to find it didn't make her self-conscious in the slightest.

"What?" Stevie asked.

Anna shook her head, tugging her gaze away to float on her back. "Nothing. Just... I never expected to be here like this with you."

"Blame Levi," Stevie grumbled, dancing weightlessly into deeper depths. Further from the shore. Further from their clothes and the car and everything that had felt real yet no longer seemed to matter. Further into shadows, where only the chirping crickets and faint breeze could find them.

"I don't mean that," Anna said. "I mean... When we were together, I thought it was forever. And then when we broke up, I didn't think I'd ever see you again. Neither of those things ended up being true. Somehow, we're both here now."

"Because you came back," Stevie pointed out, scraping her damp hair from her eyes.

"I'm glad that I did," Anna breathed.

Stevie sucked in a breath, knowing they were treading close to something that they shouldn't be. Not now. It was too late. Too complicated. Stevie didn't have the time or energy to get hurt again.

But she couldn't disagree. She couldn't shut it down, no matter how she tried — because she was glad. And no matter what happened tomorrow, or what had happened yesterday, they were here, now, in the dead of summer, wrapped in birdsong and dusk and the foul stench of a lake that had been stewing in the sun all day, and she wouldn't swap any of it for the world. She so rarely felt a peace like this. And she hadn't thought she'd ever see Anna again either, let alone swim inches from her.

And she was so beautiful.

"Me too," Stevie admitted.

Anna's lips curled with a pleased smile, water kissing her chest, her collarbone, as she inched closer still. Her hand rose from the water to tuck Stevie's short hair behind her ear carefully. As though frightened that a sudden movement might make Stevie recoil. Stevie wasn't sure if it would yet.

When her eyes fluttered shut, though, Anna came closer still, hands clinging to the rippling hem of her tunic on the water.

"I did miss you," Anna whispered. "And I am sorry."

Stevie didn't know if she believed it. She wanted to. But she couldn't let herself, not completely. Not when she knew that she had caused their rift too and couldn't yet find it in her to explain why.

She bowed her head and moved away, glan-

cing to the shore. She had to go back. She had to remind herself of all of the reasons why she couldn't
fall in love with Anna again, if she had even ever
stopped. But it was difficult with Anna's grey eyes
burning into her and the straps of her bra slipping off her sun-browned shoulders and the way
her tongue slid across the seam of her lips to catch
droplets from her Cupid's bow.

Maybe Stevie could pretend for a few more
moments.

Maybe she could ask questions she'd always
been afraid to ask before. "Did you? Did you think
of me when you were busy in Cardiff?"

"All the time." Anna didn't hesitate, and it
took Stevie aback. She tried not to show it.

"I always imagined you with someone else,"
Stevie admitted, voice strained. "Someone like
you: career-driven and always distracted and very
fond of blazers."

Anna snorted at that, her nose wrinkling.
"Are those my best qualities?"

Stevie shrugged, waiting for her to answer.

Finally, she did. "There was no one else."

"Never?" Stevie found it hard to believe.

But Anna shook her head, and Stevie found
herself believing it. She had never lied before. She
had no reason to now. "I dated, but nothing serious. Not like us. I sometimes wondered if maybe
that was it for me. I'm just supposed to have one
real shot at love, and... Well, I blew it."

Stevie's heart tightened to a solid, twisting,

agonising mass behind her ribs. "I don't think that's how it works."

Anna splashed her lightly, droplets sprinkling from her fingernails. "No? You found someone, then?"

Glaring, Stevie pushed the water back. "No. I don't have time for that anymore. But I'd like to think that when I'm ready again, it'll come around."

Except she knew it didn't work like that either. She wasn't ready yet. But, somehow, swimming in this lake with Anna felt like a second chance. An opportunity to fix things. One she couldn't afford to take.

Anna's eyes glistened. They were close again, noses almost brushing. The shore disappeared. Everything disappeared but this: her.

And then panic. Memories of Stevie stifling sobs in the shower because her father was sick and Anna had broken her apart. She couldn't do it again. She couldn't.

"It's cold. We should get back." She pulled away, wading back towards the sand and the gravel and the trees, water dragging down her limbs and tunic and the warm air fanning her damp skin with its sticky, inescapable breath. The loamy earth slipped unpleasantly between her toes and stayed there.

She hadn't thought this next part through. She couldn't dry off with her tunic clinging to her, and she couldn't get dressed still sopping wet. She

glanced over her shoulder, spotted Anna's lean silhouette approaching, and huffed.

The tunic was a pain to peel off, even worse
knowing Anna was probably watching, but she
had no choice. She tried to do it as quickly as she
could, letting her bare torso exposed to the muggy
night for only a moment before she wrapped the
towel around herself.

Anna reached her side and took a towel of
her own to dry herself down.

Stevie attempted to step into her jogging
bottoms. It didn't work. Then, she tried to keep the
towel secured with one hand while she shimmied
into her pants with the other, but with her skin
still tacky and already gathering sweat again, they
refused to budge.

A curse fell from her as she nearly dropped
the towel, and then Anna had clutched her own
hands around it. "Let me hold it. I'm not looking,
promise."

She wasn't, her lids sealed shut obediently.
Stevie surrendered the towel, making sure that the
makeshift curtain remained between them. With
a sigh, she tugged up her joggers and then pulled
on her tank top before slipping her shoes back on.

"Thank you," she said, pulling the towel
back.

Anna didn't ask for the same courtesy, but
then, what was the point when she'd already
stripped off in front of Stevie? She dressed quickly,
twisting her hair into a loose bun. "Let's go."

They walked back to camp in silence, feet crunching through foliage and an owl hooting somewhere in the distance. Stevie looked up. She could just glimpse the stars twinkling through slivers of space in the trees, and they made her feel smaller. Not as important. As though she could fall in love again and be okay in the end, so long as the universe was bigger than all of them. She could be heartbroken or bleeding or turned to ash, but the stars would always matter more.

It was just like Anna to interrupt Stevie's profound reflection with a yelp. "Barnacles! Bloody, bloody barnacles!"

Stevie whipped around to find her crouched on the floor, cradling her knee. "What happened?"

"I think I tripped over a tree root." Anna tried to straighten her leg and winced. Her trousers had torn across the knee, a bloody gash visible beneath the frayed material. "I'm okay. Just dopey and terrible at camping."

Lines etched themselves into Stevie's forehead as she crouched beside Anna. "Can you walk?"

"I think so. It's only a graze." It looked a little bit deeper than a graze even in the shadows, but Stevie didn't think it helpful to say so. With her hand locked around Anna's upper arm, Stevie pulled Anna to her feet, glad to find she could at least straighten and bend her knees.

"I have a first aid kit in my tent."

Anna choked on her own amusement. "Of

course you do."

"You can stay here and bleed if you'd prefer."

"So sympathetic." Anna rolled her eyes and they walked back to camp together, led by an orange glow in the shadows. Only embers were left of the fire, Quentin and Levi nowhere to be seen, though it couldn't have been that late. Stevie let Anna into their tent first and then, out of habit, scrambled in to check her phone. There was still no signal, and it left her uneasy. She didn't like being far away from her father, not knowing how he was.

But she couldn't think of that now.

Instead, she lit a lantern as Anna shuffled over to make room, inspecting her wound. Stevie didn't miss the scowl that she directed at their thinly-walled bedroom for the night.

"I still don't understand camping. We could have stayed in a hotel."

"And have a good, luxurious night's sleep?" Stevie asked as she rooted through her backpack for the travel-size first aid kit. "Where's the fun in that?"

"Complimentary bathrobes and a hot shower. Disgusting." Anna clucked her tongue sarcastically, and Stevie turned back with the kit in hand to find her rosy-cheeked and smirking.

Biting down on her smile, Stevie found some iodine to clean the wound with, as well as a collection of gauze and plasters spilling out onto her sleeping bag. "Alright. Let's have a look."

Anna pulled at the hole in her trousers, but there was no way Stevie could do anything in such a small gap. She sighed impatiently.

"Roll them up."

"They don't roll up," Anna said. "They're skinny-fit."

"Then pull them down."

Anna narrowed her eyes and shuffled awkwardly in the small space to shimmy out of her trousers. "If you wanted me to get naked again, you only had to ask."

"You're very witty tonight. Are you feeling alright?" Stevie pressed her palm to Anna's forehead as though checking her temperature.

"Maybe you bring it out of me." Anna's eyes sparkled until Stevie felt as though she'd been lit on fire.

With a shake of her head, Stevie used the water from her flask to wet a fistful of gauze and pressed it to Anna's bare leg. It was already sticky with congealed blood, the gash relatively deep. If she hadn't seen plenty of injuries like this with her father and his falls and the clumsy twins, she might have been fazed.

Anna, on the other hand, hissed in pain, drawing her knee away. "*Ow!*"

"Oh, don't be a baby," Stevie scolded. Her fingers curled around Anna's calf to pull it back, and then she attempted to clean the wound — this time, with an iron grip. Anna's skin was somehow both prickly and soft, hot and cold, and Stevie tried not to think about how close they were.

And how half-naked Anna was.

Anna groused again but stayed put. "It hurts, you know."

Stevie dabbed the wound as gently as she could. "You'll survive."

"And now I won't be able to wear a skirt."

"Tragic."

It had stopped bleeding, but the fibres in the gauze clung to the shredded piece of skin and the area around it was still an angry shade of red. Stevie stuck the largest plaster she could find across Anna's knee and then secured it with another two in case they tried to budge overnight. Having any clothes stuck to it in the morning wouldn't be pleasant.

"There," she said, and yet did not tear her hands away from Anna's leg. "All done."

"You didn't have to do this," Anna whispered. "Thank you."

Stevie shrugged without making eye contact. "I'm used to it."

A pause. And then: "Because of your dad?"

Stevie squeezed her eyes closed. She didn't want to talk about her dad now. She didn't want to lie awake tonight worrying about him. To distract herself, because it was all she could do, she put the kit away and washed her hands with anti-bacterial gel quickly.

Anna cleared her throat behind her. "Sorry. I didn't mean to upset you."

"You didn't. Did you still want to sleep top and tail?"

Anna only shrugged, but Stevie didn't see what other option they had. She wasn't sure what would happen if they slept side by side tonight. Before she found out, she pulled her pillows down to the opposite end of the tent and slipped into her sleeping bag.

It was comfortable for all of two seconds, and then she began to sweat again and kicked the blanket off her legs. A moment later, an airless wind caused the frail walls to ripple and the zips of the tent danced across Stevie's face. She groaned in frustration.

"What?" asked Anna.

Stevie didn't reply, not until another breeze rippled through the tent and left the zip poking into her eye. She huffed dramatically and sat up, finding Anna lying on her side with her head resting against her hand. She still had not put her trousers back on.

"I'm not sleeping down there."

"Okay."

"We can make a pillow wall."

"Stevie," Anna sighed. "Do we really have to? After everything we've been through together, has it really come to pillow walls?"

Stevie supposed it *was* a bit ridiculous. They were both adults. They could sleep beside one another for one or two nights and not tear each other's clothes off.

Then again, they were already halfway there — and it was very, very hot even without the sun beating down on them.

"Fine," Stevie pouted. "But I'm taking my pants off, too. I'm too hot."

"Good," Anna said, and then: "Not good like that. I don't mean I want you to take off your pa — oh, forget it."

Stevie kicked off her joggers and then tried to settle again, flipping her pillow to the cooler side and turning her back to Anna. She felt Anna ease down beside her, could smell the light layer of sweat, lakewater, and diluted perfume on her skin, and was very aware of the fact that she was bare and on show from the waist down aside from modest, plain black underwear.

"Stevie?"

"Hmm?" Stevie hummed.

"Thank you," Anna mumbled. "For taking care of my knee, I mean. I don't really like blood."

"I remember." It was why Stevie had tried to poke fun of her instead of drawing attention to the gooey blood as she'd cleaned it, though Anna hadn't shown a hint of unease. Always so stoic.

Stevie tried to resist the temptation to turn over and face her, but in the end, against Anna's soft breaths fanning her back, it didn't work. She did it slowly, cautiously, as though she was waiting for her body to change its mind.

It never did.

Anna was already facing her, knees to her

chest and eyes still wide open. She closed her eyes when she found Stevie looking. A moment later, she opened them again and Stevie shut hers to pretend as though she hadn't been staring. And then Stevie opened them and Anna's own veiny lids shuttered again, and they played this game until the heaviness of sleep blanketed Stevie and she could no longer pry open her lids.

The image of Anna, half-naked and looking at her like she used to, remained tattooed on her mind's eye, though, and when Anna brushed Stevie's hair from her cheek gently after tranquil moments of nothing but comfortably co-existing, Stevie pretended she was asleep just to let her.

Nine

Stevie didn't touch her phone again that weekend — not until the car ride home, when the signal returned and a barrage of pinging notifications sliced through the tranquility she'd shared with Anna.

Dread dropped through her as though she had been plunged headfirst into icy waters. She rifled through her purse with trembling fingers, Anna halting the beat she had been tapping on the steering wheel to frown beside her.

"Everything okay?"

"I don't know." Stevie hoped so. But she knew better. She'd felt the same, oily fear crawling over her skin the first time she'd gotten a phone call, when she'd been in the middle of a lecture and her mother had told her about the stroke. She'd left campus the next day and never gone back.

Too afraid to read the text messages first, Stevie called her mum and pressed the phone to her ear. Anna turned the volume dial on the car stereo, silencing the crackling radio station that had been playing.

"Mum?" Stevie asked as soon as the call was answered.

"Stevie. Where the hell are you? Why didn't you pick up?"

Despite her anxiety, a pang of bitterness shot through her — not for her mother or father, but just because. Why did she have to be readily available in case something bad happened? Why couldn't she just have one weekend away from it all? "I was camping. I didn't have any signal. What is it? What's wrong?"

"It's your dad. He's in the hospital."

The world stilled. The car's movement slowed. Even Anna seemed not to be breathing anymore. Stevie had feared the worst, and it had happened. She managed to croak out, "Why?"

A sigh on the other end of the line. She imagined Bryn on the verge of tears, perhaps standing in a waiting room or brightly lit ward, Jack lying in the next room. "He had another stroke."

"*No*." Stevie squeezed her eyes shut before they could fill with tears, resting her head against the cold windowpane. She was vaguely aware of Anna's hand finding hers, the pad of her thumb tracing soft circles into her knuckles. "Is he okay? Is he… ?"

She couldn't finish that sentence.

"I don't think he'll bounce back so easily this time, love." Bryn's voice was brittle, fragile, on the very cusp of breaking. "The doctors think it's time to put him in a hospice, at least while he recovers."

Stevie knew what that meant. She had been dreading it for years, now, a promise that always loomed like a dark raincloud. But Jack was still so young. Barely even fifty-five. How could it be time? "Okay. I'm on my way home. I'll meet you at the hospital."

"Alright, love. Text me when you're close."

"I will. Bye, Mum."

Bryn hung up, but Stevie couldn't bring herself to lower the phone for painful seconds, minutes afterwards. Anna was still holding her hand, glancing at her with concern glistening in her eyes.

"What is it?" she asked quietly. "What's happened?"

Stevie couldn't keep it from Anna anymore. She knew that. There was no way she could pretend to be okay for the next hour, and she didn't have it in her to try. She swallowed the lump in her throat and stared at the grey, endless motorway ahead. "My dad had another stroke. He's in hospital. They want to move him to a hospice."

"*Another*?" Anna's brows furrowed, grip tightening. "I didn't know..." She trailed off as though realizing.

"His first was eight years ago."

"Oh." A moment of excruciating pause. "So when you dropped out of uni..."

"Yeah." Stevie couldn't breathe. Couldn't think. It was a wonder she didn't come apart at the seams. She tried to focus on the seatbelt keeping her upright and whole in the car seat, the cushion beneath her thighs, Anna's warm hand in her cold one still. All of these things tethering her to now, keeping her here rather than the hollow vacuum teetering somewhere close.

"You should have said, Stevie," Anna whispered, throat bobbing and eyes glistening with tears. Stevie's own remained dry. If she let herself feel too much, if she let herself cry, she wouldn't ever stop. "If I'd have known —"

"I didn't have a choice," Stevie said. "I had to come back. But you didn't, and you made it clear you wouldn't. That's just the way it was."

"I made a mistake. I should have talked to you first."

"It doesn't matter now."

"It matters to *me*." Anna's voice strained like an elastic band pulled tight. "You needed me and —"

And all of that heartbreak and abandonment and loss seemed to erupt in Stevie's chest, the smoke pouring through the slats of her ribs and rising like bile in her throat as she ripped her hand from Anna's.

Needed her? She didn't *need* anyone. She never had. She had coped all on her own, refusing to break. She had built a business from the ground while caring for her father. It was an insult to suggest otherwise. To suggest that she couldn't live without Anna, as though her whole life revolved around her after eight years of not knowing where she was or why she'd left.

"I didn't *need* you. I never *needed* you."

Anna winced. "I didn't mean it that way. I'm sorry."

"*You* left *me*," Stevie said, voice thick with rage. "I wasn't going to chase you or bring you back kicking and screaming. You made your choice, Anna, and I made mine. Don't ever think I couldn't live without you."

"I don't think that." Anna shook her head and veered into the next lane. "And you're right. You didn't need me. But maybe... Maybe I needed you."

Stevie frowned, bewildered. "You *had* me."

Anna sighed. "But when you dropped out without telling anyone, it wasn't just me who made a choice. You did, too. You left without telling me why, Stevie. You made that decision alone. How was I supposed to know why?

"You're right. You didn't need me and I knew it, and when you disappeared so suddenly, I realised that maybe I wasn't a vital component of your life anymore. Because when you love someone, you work it out together. You tell each other things. And yet we were both guilty of keeping all of the bad things to ourselves. Me with my mum, you with your dad. We stopped *talking* somewhere along the line, didn't we?"

The fire in Stevie's chest calmed against Anna's gentle, rational words. She was right. Of course she was right. For all of Anna's flaws, Stevie had only done the same. Maybe they'd been too proud. Too young. Too immature. But their secrecy, the way they had cut themselves off from one another when things got difficult, that had broken them. It was just as much Stevie's fault as it was Anna's.

"I suppose we did."

Anna pursed her lips as though in pain. "I wish we hadn't."

Stevie wished the same, though she couldn't stand to admit it. She only sat back in her seat and crossed her legs, wondering what she was returning home to. She knew what strokes could do to someone. She knew how sick her father already was. She sighed and pinched the bridge of her nose, a throb beginning to awaken like a drumbeat in her head.

"Could you drop me off at the hospital on the way back?" Stevie asked finally.

"Of course. Would... Would you like me to stay with you?"

Stevie did. She wanted nothing more than to hold Anna's hand and fix all of the mistakes they'd made the first time around. But they weren't those people anymore, and she wouldn't make Anna suffer through whatever it was she was about to endure. "You don't have to."

"I want to." Anna's hand returned to Stevie's as though it belonged there. It didn't sound like a lie either.

So, Stevie squeezed Anna's fingers and forced a shaky smile. To right old wrongs. To open a part of herself that had always remained locked up before now. Because Anna wanted to be there and Stevie wanted to let her, and maybe they were different, but maybe that was why it seemed easier than it ever had been before.

"Okay."

∞∞∞

Anna didn't ask why Stevie wanted to be dropped off at the shop instead of home. She didn't feel it was her place to ask. She had only been able to hold Stevie's hand and make sure she knew she was there when they visited Jack, who had been drawn and pale and faraway, with tubes knitted through his arms. He hadn't been able to remember Stevie's name, let alone Anna's.

Anna followed Stevie through the curtain of hanging beads now, the subtle scent of incense and old, dusty wood greeting them. It was too quiet. At least in the car, there had been the faint purr of the engine. Anna didn't know what to do without it. She hovered as Stevie collapsed into a chair behind the counter and mechanically began to flick through paperwork. Invoices, Anna saw. Bills.

"I'm sure that can wait."

Stevie abandoned them and wandered over to her work table instead, where half-finished wood carvings and wall hangings sat.

"Stevie."

"I only have fifteen done," she muttered. "Marigold wants thirty."

"You have time, yet."

"Not really. I've barely made a start on the wall hangings. And a huge Etsy order came in yesterday."

"So, start tomorrow," Anna suggested gently, hand rubbing small circles along Stevie's spine. "It can wait. You've had a long day."

Stevie lowered, bracing her elbows against the worktop and bowing her head. "It can't wait."

"Of course it ca —"

"I think I have to close the shop," she blurted, voice cracked and thick with tears. The first ones she'd let fall all day. Anna felt them as though they were her own. "I'm barely scraping by, and there's so much work to do, and my dad needs me, and I can't do it all on my own anymore. I can't, Anna. I can't."

She kept repeating it: "*I can't.*"

Each time it felt like an arrow slicing through Anna's chest. She wanted to make it better, and yet had no idea how. Stevie had been carrying so much on her shoulders for so long, always convinced it was her burden alone to bear. But Anna couldn't let her do it anymore. Not without her.

Gently, she tugged Stevie into her chest and curled her arms around Stevie's soft frame, the smell of the woods and the campfire still clinging to the clothes she hadn't changed.

"You can," Anna whispered, fingers tangling in Stevie's golden, feathery hair. "You can, love. You're not alone. I'm here now. And your dad is going to get the help he needs. It's not your job anymore."

"I don't know what my mum will do without him," admitted Stevie, tears dampening Anna's shoulders. "She needs me too."

Anna couldn't bear it anymore. She pulled away, cupping Stevie's jaw until her tears spilled across Anna's fingers and Stevie was forced to look at her. "But that doesn't mean that you have to be there all the time, Stevie. It doesn't mean you should sacrifice everything. You've done more than enough over the years."

Stevie's eyes fell closed for a moment, sobs ebbing into sniffles. Tenderly, Anna wiped her tears with the pad of her thumb, trying not to think about how easy it would be to kiss her. How, whenever Stevie was upset when they were together, that's what Anna would do. Kiss her. Chase away the sadness by making sure she knew she was loved.

But Stevie seemed to remember too, because she nudged her nose against Anna's, hands entwining and falling between their close bodies. She repeated the gesture a moment later as though asking.

And Anna couldn't give in. Not now. Not like this. She twisted her finger through Stevie's hair again, inhaling her so that she, at least, could remind herself how it felt to be this close to Stevie. And then she stepped away, distracting herself with the hoards of shells organised in a craft box.

"You'll have to teach me how to make these wall thingies so I can help with the orders."

A mangled chuckle fell from Stevie as she wiped her eyes with her sleeve. "You don't have to. Really."

"I *want* to. I want to help however I can," Anna said. "Why don't I stick the kettle on first and then we can decide what to do?"

She made to leave, but Stevie's fingers tangling through hers pulled her back. Her face was splotchy beneath the freckles, eyes puffy, but still beautiful — and still all it took for Anna's heart to speed up. "Anna."

"Yep?"

"Thank you for everything you've done today."

Anna softened and smiled, daring to place a soft kiss on the back of Stevie's palm. Her skin was cold and laced with the clean, clinical smell of hospitals and antibacterial gel. "Of course. Always."

She meant it.

Ten

"Judith!" called Anna as she caught a glimpse of the silver-haired councillor marching through the town hall. Her kitten heels clicked against the old mosaic floors, jowls wobbling with the movement.

She didn't stop, so Anna called again, running after her now. "Judith! Do you have a moment?"

The older woman came to a standstill at last, her black leather briefcase still swinging in her hand. Anna didn't think it held anything, though the older woman carried it each day. Probably thought it made her look important.

Judith had been fine to work with at first — until she had complained about the smell of Anna's cheese sandwiches at lunchtime and lectured her about how unethical and hypocritical it was for her, an environmental development advisor, to eat dairy and contribute to the world's problems. When Anna pointed out that it was the job of million-pound corporations to promote sustainability, not individuals like Anna who didn't have time nor money to spend on vegan cheese and gluten-free breads, Judith soon shut up.

But Anna had to push that aside now, flashing the councillor her politest smile as she pulled her to one side. "I've been meaning to catch you all week."

"Oh?" Judith asked, peering over her round-framed glasses conspiratorially. "What can I help you with, Miss Conway?"

"It's about the new Coast Protection Act, actually. I plan to bring it up in this evening's meeting, but I wanted to run it by you first. I think the bylaws are a little too rigid for businesses who rely on sourcing their materials locally."

Judith pursed her lips as though she was sucking on a lemon, placing her free hand on her jutting hip impatiently. "*You* suggested putting the rules in place."

"I did," Anna nodded, "but I was new to town and unaware of the impact it would have on local business. A few shops are struggling because of it." It wasn't necessarily all true, but it wasn't a lie either. Stevie was still collecting driftwood in the dead of night, and Anna was still pretending as though she didn't know. But it meant Stevie was losing sleep that, on top of worrying about her father, who had just been transferred to Castell Bay's hospice, she couldn't afford to lose, and Anna felt guilty each time she noticed the purple circles beneath Stevie's eyes. They couldn't go on like this. Anna couldn't keep being the reason for it.

"You mean *one* shop," Judith retorted sternly. "That hippie woman who tears our beaches apart for her own gain."

Anna couldn't help but scoff. "That's a bit dramatic, Judith."

"Is it?" Judith raised a patchy, grey brow. "You said yourself that taking driftwood destroys habitats."

"I did. And it's true. But…"

"But you're going to go back on your own advice for the sake of one poor, unfortunate business owner? That's not very professional."

"I'm sorry if that's the way you see it," Anna sighed, patience fraying, "but we have to look at this from every angle."

"And we have. Our concerns for coastal habitats remain. Look, Miss Conway, I know you are new at your job." Judith stepped closer until Anna could smell the foul taste of morning-old coffee on her breath. "Take it from your elders. You can't please everyone, no matter how hard you try. Your job is to worry about the environment, not businesses. Now, let's not have this conversation again."

Anna flexed her fingers so tightly that the plastic edge of her binder bit into her palms. She wasn't new at her job at all. She had gone from graduation straight into an internship and never looked back. Still, somehow she managed to sweep her ponytail off her shoulder and grin amiably.

"Some councillors would believe they've failed their job when their policies cost people their livelihood." Her voice dripped with the false compliment. She could play Judith's game. She could be curt, underhand, and pompous too. "I admire your... natural ability to disregard your neighbours and friends."

With that, Anna sauntered away, spine stiff and burning against Judith's stare. She didn't have to turn around to know it was there. To know that, in having the last word, she had left the arrogant councillor flabbergasted. If only she had eyes in the back of her head to see the reaction firsthand.

But Anna wouldn't waste another moment on Judith. She would find another way to get Stevie her materials. She would find a way to right all of her wrongs.

But first, she would have to go home and prepare for a, no doubt, tense dinner with her parents.

Eleven

Stevie knocked on the glossy, white-painted door of Anna's apartment, a bottle of cheap wine from Irene's convenience store clutched in her free hand. With the clanging it caused, Stevie thought she might have overdone it a bit with the decorative knuckle rings.

She didn't know why that mattered. It was just a dinner. She was glad to do something normal after a week of hospital visits and hospice plans. Jack had been moved to Castell Bay's main hospice yesterday, and ever since Stevie had been trying not to think of how small and frail he had looked beneath a pile of Bryn's crocheted blankets.

But she didn't *feel* normal. She felt like she was meeting Anna's parents again for the first time, only this time with alcohol instead of lemonade, because apparently they were adults now. It was ridiculous, really. She'd seen more of Jen and Daniel Conway these past few years than Anna probably had.

The door swung open, wafting with it the heady, floral scent of Anna's perfume. Her dark hair had been straightened to her shoulders, making her features look sharper, like her mother's.

Her dress was not patterned with the usual polka dots or flowers, instead a simple black that would have made her look a little bit like a lawyer had she not been fidgeting so much.

Anna was nervous. Nervous, and still so completely hellbent on pleasing Jen by changing herself.

"Oh." Anna's grey eyes widened at the sight of Stevie. "I didn't think you'd come."

"You asked me to," Stevie reminded with a sheepish smile. Was she not *supposed* to have come? Had Anna just asked to be polite?

"I know. I'm glad you did. It's just... I know you have a lot on your plate. I wouldn't have blamed you if you skipped dinner with my parents."

Stevie shrugged. She did still have an awful lot of orders to catch up on downstairs, but Anna had been helping her most evenings, and she'd been right about her father: he was receiving around the clock palliative care, now, which left little room for Stevie's old responsibilities. Bryn had been floating around the house like a ghost too, their purposes stripped with Jack's departure. So much of their life had become caring for him that they were no longer sure who to be now. All Stevie had to worry about at present was making rent on time, and to do that, she needed to get Marigold's order finished by next weekend.

"A promise is a promise," she said, handing Anna the wine. "Your mum won't like that, by the way. It cost four pounds from the off-licence."

"Good." Anna placed the bottle on the kitchen counter and hooked a set of silver earrings
through her lobes. "I love the face she makes when
she drinks cheap wine. You didn't have to, though.
Thank you, Stevie."

"It's no problem." Stevie smiled softly, lean-
ing against the counter so that the heat of the oven
hit her shins. She sniffed for some telltale sign as
to what was cooking, finding only hints of garlic
and herbs. "What are we eating tonight?"

"Oh, just some chicken tarragon recipe I cop-
ied off Nigella Lawson," Anna waved off, slipping
on a pair of black pumps and adjusting the already
pin-straight cutlery set out on the small dining
table. She must have spent hours working on the
apartment this week. It had still been empty and
everything boxed up last time Stevie had visited,
but now it looked like a home, with a new, vel-
vet couch and matching armchair in the open-
plan living room and potted plants in each corner.
Stevie would have to ask for tips on how not to
kill them. Her own banana leaf plant had wilted
awfully. Probably because she had not watered it
since Christmas.

"Oh." Stevie bit her lip hesitantly.

"What?"

"It's just… Well, I'm a vegetarian."

Anna's face fell as though the wind had been
knocked out of her, her hand slapping her forehead. "Oh, barnacles. Of course."

Despite her embarrassment for not telling Anna sooner, Stevie couldn't help but stifle a laugh. "It's okay. I'll eat around the meat."

"No. I'm sure I can make you pasta or something. Just hang on…."

Anna tried to brush past her, and without thinking, Stevie reached out to hold her hands.

"Anna," she chided gently, appreciatively, because Anna was flustered, her eyebrows puckered, and it was both adorable and difficult to see. "It's fine. Really."

"It's not fine," said Anna. "It won't be, anyway. My mum will pick at every little thing she can. This will just be another way I'm useless."

Stevie's heart wrenched, and her grip tightened. When she pulled Anna close, it came too naturally, too easily, and she tried not to think about what it meant. Why, ever so slowly, they were falling back into old habits — and not questioning them or talking about them aloud. "Well, your mum's wrong, and I am very good at stealthily spitting chicken into a napkin, so she won't have to know."

"But you'll still be hungry."

Stevie pointed to the bowl of buttered, crusty bread already sitting out. "Carbs."

With a smirk, Anna tilted her head. "Are you sure?"

"Yes, I'm sure. It'll all be perfect. Promise." Their fingers laced together, their twining hands a duet they'd been left to improvise. Anna's skin was warm and smooth and familiar, a mould Stevie had always been the right shape to fill.

But that wasn't a good idea, Stevie reminded herself. Where she had once believed it, that inner voice of hers only sounded mechanical and unconvinced now. A rusty defence no longer quick or powerful enough to keep out the enemy.

"Stevie...." Anna whispered, but whatever she was about to say was interrupted by a knock on the door. She paled and tucked her hair behind her ears, smoothing out her dress. "Okay. They're here."

"You're going to be fine," Stevie reassured a final time. "I'm your buffer, remember?"

Anna nodded, though it was absent. She wasn't listening anymore. She wandered over to the door and opened it, engulfed immediately by a set of broad arms.

"I've got a bone to pick with you, lady." It was her father, Daniel, who greeted her so warmly. Jen held back with her hands clasped in front of her, rocking on her heels. "Where on earth have you been?"

"Cardiff." Anna's answer was muffled by her father's large frame, but Stevie didn't think she imagined the way it wavered with emotion. She felt awful for her. To separate herself from the only loving parent Anna had because of a mistake her mother had made... Stevie couldn't imagine how hard it must have been.

"Oh, I see. Cardiff. Where phones don't work

and there are no post offices?" His voice remained light, joking, just as it always had been.

"I know. I'm sorry, Dad. It's so good to see you again."

Daniel cupped Anna's face, love swimming in his eyes and his toothy smile. "And you, sweetheart. Something's smelling good."

He stepped into the apartment, stopping when he caught sight of Stevie. "Oh, hello, Stevie! I always knew the two of you would end up together again eventually. Good to see you, love. How's your dad?"

Stevie looked to Anna for aid, but she was busy casting Jen a terse nod before taking her coat, so Stevie handled it alone. "Anna and I aren't together, Mr. Conway. Just friends. And my dad is in the hospice at the moment. He had another stroke."

"Oh no." Daniel scratched the bald patch at the crown of his head solemnly. "Sorry to hear that. Give him my best, will you?"

"Of course."

Jen sniffed, a cold gaze running up and down Stevie as she returned to Daniel's side. "I suppose a family dinner was too much to ask, Anna?"

"Stevie is family," Anna answered, crouching to check on the chicken in the oven with a pair of mitts slung across her shoulder.

Beneath Jen's glare of disapproval, Stevie thought it a good time to bring out the cheap alcohol. "Wine, anyone?"

"White or red?" Jen asked.

Stevie checked the bottle. The colour fit neither description. "Er, pink?"

"Rosé? Dear me, I thought only single mothers whose lives revolve around brunch drank that."

"Nope, it's popular among us spinsters who eat plain old breakfasts and lunches too." Stevie's smile dripped with sarcasm as she uncorked the bottle. It released the fruity, vinegary stench of cheap wine, and Stevie fought the strong urge to throw it all over Jen.

"Very well." Jen sighed. "If there's nothing else on offer, you may as well pour me a glass."

After searching for the glasses in the relatively empty cupboards, Stevie did just that — making sure, of course, that both hers and Jen's were almost full. She would need it to get through this night without spewing a few harsh words Jen's way.

"The chicken is dry."

Anna stiffened in her chair against the first of her mother's criticisms. The chicken wasn't dry at all. The chicken was slathered in oil and herbs, just as Nigella Lawson had instructed on the television, and it had been in the oven for the right amount of time. She had stopped arguing with her mother a long time ago, though, so Anna merely speared a stick of asparagus with her fork and nibbled on the end.

"Is it? I was just going to say it's lovely." Stevie cast Anna a supportive look from beside her. Their chairs were so close that their thighs brushed each time one of them shifted slightly, and Stevie was so far doing a good job of chopping the meat up to make it look as though she'd eaten some.

"Tastes fine to me, love," Daniel agreed, chomping away as though he'd never been fed.

"So... Anna. What is it you do at the town hall? Judith tells me she's been working with you quite a lot these past few weeks," Jen said, dabbing the corners of her puckered mouth on her napkin. It came away with pale red lip gloss. "Of course, chatting with other people is the only way I learn about these things at all. So nice of you to keep me in the loop."

Anna sighed, knife scraping across ceramic as she sawed at her chicken. Maybe it *was* a bit dry, just in the middle. "I'm a policy and economic development advisor for the village council."

"Long job titles always sound so terribly boring."

"*Jen*," Daniel scolded. Despite his kind words so far, something terrible and foreign sparked in his eyes tonight: anger. Anna couldn't yet tell if it was directed at her or Jen.

"I'm only saying. All that debt you must be

in from university. Was it worth it?"

"I enjoy my job, Mum," Anna said, jaw clenching. "And what about you? Do you still work the office telephones for Mr. Paisley?"

"I got a raise last year, thank you very much. I'll be able to retire early and jet off somewhere hot soon."

"Good for you," she smiled.

The sarcasm was met with an earsplitting clattering of cutlery. Jen had thrown down her knife and fork and now glared at Anna, a vein pulsing beneath the papery skin of her temple. "Enough of this. I think I've been quite good to give you another chance after you neglected us for eight years, so the least you can do is treat us with respect."

"*Jen*," Daniel ground out again, but Anna wasn't listening to any of it.

Stevie's warm hand had found hers under the table, and they rested together on top of Anna's thigh. She squeezed, giving Anna a strength she hadn't known she'd needed. Nothing had changed, even now. Stevie was still holding her hand while her mother laid into her.

"Why do you hate us, Anna?" Jen continued, rising in volume and pitch. "What have we possibly done to deserve it?"

Anna gulped down a deep, ragged breath. "You know the answer to that. And we're in front of guests, Mother. Please calm down."

"Oh, Stevie has been just as hostile with me

tonight. You used to be a lovely girl. Our Anna must have poisoned you."

"*Excuse me*?" Stevie replied incredulously. "Has it ever occurred to you that perhaps *you're* the poison here?"

Anna stopped breathing for a moment, then. Everyone did. It grew so quiet that Anna could hear the gulls bathing in the guttering outside.

Stevie was right. Of course she was. But Anna had never been brave enough to say so, and Daniel had grown pale. Flames flickered in her mother's irises like fire spreading across gasoline-soaked concrete.

Jen broke the silence first. "Well? Are any of you going to jump to my defense?"

With a huff, Daniel dabbed his damp, sun-kissed forehead with his serviette and locked eyes with Anna. There was no anger there. No resentment, though there should have been. He had been inadvertently punished by something Jen had done. Anna had abandoned him because she was too afraid to tell him the truth.

"I want to know what happened. How did we get here? I know it was something. I know there's something the two of you are holding onto."

"I should go." Stevie rose to leave, but Anna pulled her back down.

"No. Stay." It was almost a plea. She lifted her eyes cautiously to Jen, then, burning beneath Daniel's stare. "Mum? Are you going to tell him?"

"Tell me what?" Daniel asked.

Jen remained still as stone, and just as sharp-edged with her high cheekbones and pointy chin. A familiar warning shadowed those already dark features.

But how much longer could Anna pay it heed? Her dad was right. It should never have gotten this far and he was owed the truth, no matter how badly it hurt.

She cleared her throat, clinging onto Stevie for dear life as she mustered a courage that had been pushed into black, cobwebbed corners for too long. "Alright. I can't keep doing this. I left because Mum cheated on you, Dad."

Another bout of silence. And then Daniel guffawed as though he found the words quite entertaining. Anna wondered if he'd gone mad as he slapped his knee. But then he said, "That's common knowledge, love. I already know."

"You…" Anna frowned, wiping her free, clammy hand on her dress. "You knew?"

Jen's cheeks blazed, but she said nothing, did nothing. Just sat there and let them talk about it as though she was not the villain of the story. Maybe she truly didn't care. Maybe she never would.

"Yes, I knew," Daniel confirmed. "I'm not an idiot."

"For how long?"

"Long enough. Is this why you haven't spoken to us for so long, Anna?"

A warm brush against Anna's leg as Stevie shuffled closer. A reminder that she was there, still.

"I… I was…"

"Anna," Jen warned.

And Anna understood. Whatever Daniel knew, he hadn't *always* known. Not when Anna was still living in their home. Not when she'd walked in on it as it happened. Jen must have conveniently omitted the lies and manipulation thrown Anna's way.

"I was told to keep it a secret," Anna admitted, and though the words broke in her throat, shards of glass scraping raw skin, it felt as though a weight had been lifted and she was finally free. No more lies. No more guilt. No more of this. "She told me I couldn't tell you. I should have. I know I should have. But I didn't want to be the one to break your heart like that. I couldn't have that on my shoulders. So, I ran away."

Anna saw the moment Daniel crumbled. He turned to Jen with shattered eyes, lower lip wobbling. "Is that true, Jen? Did you get her involved in this?"

Jen scowled. "I didn't involve her in anything."

"I walked in on them," said Anna. "I saw it happen. That was why she asked me to lie."

She didn't think she'd ever seen her father upset before. Not when his mother died, or when Anna said farewell the day he dropped her off at university for the first time, or when he fought with Jen and she threatened divorce. Not like this.

"How could you?" he asked Jen. "How could you do that to our daughter?"

"It wasn't intentional."

Daniel banged his fist against the table, causing the plates to quiver and the floral centre-piece to toppel. Beside Anna, Stevie startled. Her father said, "Getting caught wasn't, perhaps. But asking her to lie? Letting it fester between the two of you for eight years? I asked you time and time again why you wouldn't reach out to her. Why I never saw my daughter anymore. You said you didn't know, that you had tried. You lied every time."

"Anna was stubborn." Jen crossed her arms over her chest firmly. "She made it clear she wasn't interested in having us in her life."

"Because of *you*!" Daniel shook his head in disbelief, eyes turning watery. "I'm sorry, Anna. I'm so, so sorry. You did right by staying well away from us. You deserved better."

"*I'm* sorry." Anna's cheeks were damp now, chest bursting with pain. "I'm so sorry, Dad."

Rising from his chair, Daniel made his way over, cupping Anna's cheek with his calloused palm. She had missed it. Missed her father. "It was never your fault, love. *Never*."

She'd had no idea just how much she'd needed to hear those words until they sliced through the air, through her. Years of hating herself for not telling him, for wondering if he'd ever know… they all amounted to this, here, now. And it gave her a closure she'd never expected to get.

She could breathe again. Even when everything else was exploding around her, she could breathe again.

"I love you," Anna whispered.

Daniel cast her a sad smile. "I love you too." And then he stepped back with the stiff upper lip he'd always had before, straightening his lopsided blazer and avoiding Jen's gaze. "I think I'll stay with my brother for a few days. And I think after that, Jen, you and I might talk about getting a divorce."

Jen scoffed as though he had said something funny. "Don't be absurd, Daniel."

But Daniel was no longer listening. He was walking away, as he should have years ago. Anna had never been prouder of him. She would call him tomorrow and find a way to fix things between them. Tonight, though, she cast her mother a steely glare, prying her hand from Stevie's to stand.

"I think you should leave too."

Her mother's lips twisted with disgust, but she rose, looking slightly smaller than she had walking in. Good. She deserved a taste of her own medicine. "You must be happy now."

"I'll be happy when you get out of my apartment," said Anna steadily.

And it was clear that everything was terribly wrong tonight, because for the first time in her life, Jen listened to her daughter. She walked out of the door without another word.

∞∞∞

Stevie didn't want to be the first to break the silence after Jen had slammed the door shut, but after excruciating moments of nothing but watching Anna's eyes gleam with tears, she couldn't do it anymore.

"I'm sorry. I shouldn't have said what I did to your mum." Even if she'd meant it. Even if Jen was the most poisonous person Stevie had ever met.

Anna seemed to spring to life at her words, wiping her damp cheeks and then piling plates of uneaten food to take to the sink. "It's true."

"It didn't help things."

"Well, tonight was never going to go well, was it?" She turned on the tap, water streaming out in uneven spurts. A dishwasher sat under the counter, but Anna scrubbed with a scourer until her hands were bright red from the water's temperature and covered in lemony suds.

"Anna." Stevie sighed softly. "We can talk about it if you want to. I'm here for you."

"We *are* talking about it."

"You know what I mean."

Anna stilled, throwing the sponge into the washing bowl so that it floated on the soapy surface. "I don't think I have anything left to say," she admitted quietly, voice cracking in a way that sent sympathy lancing through Stevie. "I've waited for so long for the truth to come out. Now it has, I just feel... hollow. Maybe even relieved. How can I feel that way?"

"Because you've had to deal with it alone for too many years," Stevie said, her hands clasping around Anna's damp wrist. The water dropped from her fingers onto her dress, leaving patches of dark, but Stevie didn't care. She didn't care about anything but Anna, and to show it, she inched closer. Anna had been there for her after her father's stroke. It was her turn, now. They were making up for a past of pulling away from one another when they should have drawn each other close. "You don't have to shoulder this burden by yourself. Not anymore."

Anna's lids shuttered as though in relief, head bowing until their foreheads met. "I'm glad you were here. Thank you."

"Always." It was an echo of Anna's words. An echo of their entire relationship — because they were always there. Even when they weren't, even with a rift separating them, the love in Stevie's heart had never floated away. Anna was a permanent, certain, vital part in Stevie's life, and she always would be. First loves didn't go away. Important loves didn't either, and Anna was both of those things.

With a slight shift, their noses brushed, causing heat to unfurl in Stevie's stomach again.

The same one ignited in the lake last weekend. The same one that always roared to life when Anna was near. It wasn't just lust but need. Want. And it wasn't just in her stomach, but her heart and her veins and her bones.

She didn't want to snuff it out. Not this time. She wanted to answer it, to let it have what it wanted. What she wanted. And when Anna, with a shaky breath, drew her in and pressed her lips to Stevie's, it seemed to sigh and spark and shiver within her. Because it had been waiting; waiting to come home.

Stevie's fingers crawled up to the warm nape of Anna's neck. She ran her tongue across the seam of Anna's lips, asking. Anna opened willingly, fingers clenching the thin material of Stevie's dress, seeking the cushioned flesh of her hips. She found it, lifted so that Stevie rose onto the counter, legs spread for Anna to slot between them. She was breathless and relieved and she knew that nothing had ever, would ever, feel as right as this. Kissing Anna came with the same bliss, the same heavy-hearted wonder, as it had eight years ago. The rest of her life could shift and change and turn to ruins, but this would always be the same in the end.

And Stevie needed that. She needed to cling onto it to keep her steady.

"I missed you," Anna whispered, twining her fingers through Stevie's short hair. She didn't pull away, as though she wanted to remain this close even when the kiss was broken. "I missed you so much, Stevie."

"I missed you, too." Tears pricked Stevie's eyes. Tears of joy and regret for the time they had wasted. But Anna had come back to her in the end, and that was worth the wait.

But then Stevie remembered the truth of it. Fear crept through her throat as she thought of how much it had hurt to lose Anna; how she had left her so easily. It might have been worth the wait, but was it worth the pain?

"I'm sorry. I don't think I can do this again." Stevie pulled away, stomach churning as surprise and disappointment flickered across Anna's features.

"Stevie —"

"Sorry," she repeated, hopping down from the counter onto heavy feet. She brushed past Anna without stopping, knowing that if Anna asked her to stay, Stevie would, and that was too dangerous.

She had no room for any more heartbreak in her life. So, she ran away before it tried to catch her again.

Twelve

Despite Stevie working beneath Anna's apartment, they were doing a good job of avoiding each other — again. It was almost as though nothing had happened; that Anna was new in town and they were just trying to save themselves the trouble of running into their old flames.

But that wasn't the truth, and Stevie knew it. She couldn't stop thinking about the kiss. When she was working, rushing to get Marigold's order done, or visiting her dad, or making dinner for Bryn, she was still remembering, with that phantom tingle of love still dancing on her lips.

It was becoming quite an inconvenience.

What was more inconvenient was that Stevie's rent was due and the deadline for Marigold's order was coming up. She was spread thin. Even working night and day, she still wouldn't have enough time or money to keep herself afloat. It didn't help that everything that could go wrong had: one of the carved lighthouses had turned out wonky, another had split down the middle, and she'd ran out of supplies halfway through the week and had to run out to get more.

Fingers quivering with irritation, she attempted to thread the string through the small hole she had punctured in a scallop-edged shell for the fourth time and then cursed when it frayed into loose fibres. "Ugh!"

She swiped her sweaty bangs from her face, face flushed and flustered, and wondered if she could carry on this way. She loved the shop. She loved making unique gifts from something as mundane as sea debris and shells. But that love was dampened down under pressure, and it was so much work for a one-woman show. Getting up at dawn to collect driftwood to avoid a fine. Running the shop nine-to-five all day every day. Balancing Etsy orders with Marigold's. Was it realistic to keep doing this alone?

Paying for new employees was out of the question, either way.

Her glassy gaze fell to the corner of the shop, where the dollhouse stood. Stevie had never put it on Etsy, too attached to it to want to sell it. But if she could find a buyer, it would be worth this month's rent, at least.

Maybe it was time to let it go…

The ringing of her phone broke her from her thoughts, the tone a shrill alert slicing through the peaceful guitar acoustics playing from her Spotify. Her mother's ID lit up the screen, and as always, brought with it an inexplicable wave of dread. She had long since learned to associate Bryn's calls with terrible news, even more so now.

With a deep breath, Stevie answered the call,

placing the phone to her ear. "Hi, Mum."

"Stevie, darling. Are you busy?"

Stevie scratched her wrist with unease, and flakes of glue peeled off with her skin. She didn't like the sound of her mother's shaky voice, though it at least didn't sound too urgent. Not like last time. "I'm just working on some orders. Why? Is everything okay?"

"Your dad's nurse just rang. He's got a bit of a chest infection, they think, and he's not doing too well. I just hate to think of him all alone, so I was wondering if you might run me down."

Gulping, Stevie asked, "But is he okay?"

"I don't know, love. They couldn't tell me much."

"Alright. I'm on my way. I'll pick you up soon."

She hung up, clenching her jaw to keep her emotions at bay. It felt like one thing after another, and Stevie couldn't remember the last time she'd had a real break from it all. Even the camping trip had ended badly.

Stevie reached for her purse, making sure her car keys were still in there — and froze when she came across a Post-It note scrawled with her handwriting. Marigold was coming around later with some postcards for Stevie to sell, and she was supposed to pick up and pay for half of her order.

Rent was due next week. Stevie needed that money.

Oh, bloody hell. She had promised to babysit

the twins so that Levi could have a date night with Quentin too, and they would be dropping them off soon. Why? Why did she try to do more than she was capable of?

In her panic, the only option she could think of was to go upstairs and ask for Anna's help — if she was even home. It was only five p.m., and Stevie knew from crossing paths by accident that Anna sometimes worked until past seven. After three aggressive knocks, though, the door swung open.

Anna greeted her with a creased skirt and bare feet, hair coming loose from its neat bun. Surprise spread across her features as she took Stevie in, breathless from her sprint up the stairs and still flustered with anxiety. "Hello."

"Hi. Look, I know we haven't been talking and things are weird, but I could really do with your help if you don't mind."

Anna's brows furrowed. "Of course. What is it?"

Stevie pushed her spare set of shop keys into Anna's hand. "I have to nip out to see my dad and I was hoping you could stick around until Marigold comes by for the order. It's all boxed up and ready to go with her name written on it, so you can't miss it. You can lock up and leave when she's gone. I just don't want to keep her waiting."

"No problem. But is your dad okay?"

"I don't know," Stevie admitted sheepishly. "But I have another favour. I promised Levi I'd babysit the twins, so they'll be here in an hour or so." As Anna opened her mouth to protest, Stevie said, "Thank you, Anna. This is a big help."

"But — " Anna sighed. "Fine. No problem. I can babysit, I suppose. Is there anything else I can do?"

Stevie shook her head, already preparing to stumble back down the narrow staircase. "Just see to Marigold, babysit the twins, and lock up the shop. Marigold should be here in about half an hour. And if you have any other customers, make a note of it and leave it by the till. All the prices are labelled!"

"Okay. Bye, then!" Anna's call followed Stevie down the stairs.

All Stevie could do was rasp out, "Thank you!" a final time before rushing to her car.

∞∞∞

Marigold did arrive half an hour later, just as Stevie had said, and Anna helped her with the boxes before returning inside. And then she couldn't help herself. The craft materials were still sitting out on Stevie's desk, wall hangings and wind chimes unfinished, and after a few evenings spent helping Stevie to make them, Anna thought it only right to help her finish the orders.

That was where she stood, threading string through shells, when the twins bounded in not long later, Levi behind them.

"Oh," they said, confusion wrinkling their features. "You're not Stevie."

"You're incredibly observant," Anna teased, earning a cluck of their tongue in response. She was surprised when Ralph greeted her by throwing his arms around her waist — surprised, and heartwarmed.

"Hi, Auntie Anna!"

"Hello, you." Anna grinned, pinching Ralph's dimpled cheek before turning her attention back to Levi.

"Where is she?" they asked.

"She had to leave early. An emergency with her dad. I'm covering for her."

"Oh…" Levi chewed on their lip, hovering with their phone in their hand as though unsure what to do. "Is he okay?"

"I don't know. She didn't have time to tell me." Anna hoped so. Stevie hadn't looked devastated like the day of Jack's stroke, but her eyes had still been round with panic, and the fact she'd been rushing around and had actually asked for *help* (a rare, almost non-existent occurrence for her) said enough.

"I should call Quentin and cancel, then."

"No, don't be daft!" Anna interjected, perhaps too quickly. She wanted an excuse to be Auntie Anna, she found, and wasn't daunted to try after so much time watching Stevie take care of them. "I can watch the twins. You go on your date."

"Are you sure?" Levi glanced at her reluctantly, and Anna tried not to take offense.

"Positive. Go have fun with your husband."

"Alright… but first, you need to update me." Levi sauntered to the counter and braced themself against it.

She arched an eyebrow while Ralph jostled her hand repetitively and sang 'Old MacDonald Had A Farm', making some very questionable cow noises. "About?"

"Stevie, of course!" Levi blurted. "You two have been acting weirder than usual since the camping trip. On again, off again, on again. Are you back together yet or what?"

"No."

"Wrong answer!" Levi slapped their thighs in exasperation. "Why not?"

"Because!" Ralph said.

Anna rustled his hair appreciatively. "Exactly, Ralph. Because."

"Don't teach my son how to evade answers," Levi scolded with a glare. "I know something went down the night you two went for a swim, and I know you're still head over heels, so what's going on? Why aren't you telling me?"

"*Because*," Anna huffed again, and then bowed her head as she remembered the night they almost *had* kissed. The sheer heat and hunger that had blazed between them, Anna's hands bunching Stevie's dress and her pale thighs resting against her kitchen countertop. Anna would have given

Stevie anything that night.

But Stevie hadn't wanted it.

"Anna Conway." Levi crossed their arms sternly.

"Because… It's complicated," Anna admitted, shoulders sagging. She cupped her mouth and whispered, "We kissed," so that the children wouldn't hear.

Levi gasped and clutched their chest dramatically. "Beautiful. I knew it! And might I say, you're welcome."

"Don't get excited. Stevie said she couldn't do it again, left, and we haven't talked since. In fact, I think things are actually worse than before."

"Well, of course," tutted Levi. "Stevie has been burned by you before. She's not going to hop into your arms and sail into the sunset with you right away, no matter how badly we both want her to."

Of course. Anna hadn't even spared their past a thought when kissing Stevie, too enveloped in the desperate, spine-tingling now of it all, but Stevie would not have the same luxury. Anna had abandoned her. Had she expected for Stevie to just jump into this headfirst again with her?

"Right. Yeah." Restlessly, Anna shuffled. "That makes sense."

"Don't get all pouty. I'm not saying you don't have a chance. I'm just saying that it's going to take time, and Stevie needs to feel secure with you. She's not like she used to be, wearing her heart on her sleeve. She's cautious now, especially..." Levi trailed off, but Anna knew well enough what they were going to say. *Especially with you.*

"So, how do I make her feel that way? Secure?"

They shrugged. "Be honest with her. Stick around. Show her you care and you're not going to up and leave again."

Anna didn't know how to do any of that. She was already trying her best, and caring about Stevie had always been second nature. But she would do whatever it took. She would show Stevie anyway she could. She wasn't ready to let her go a second time.

"I intend to." She nodded, determination hardening her features.

Levi squealed and tapped her nose affectionately. "I knew this day would come. You're all grown up. I'm so proud."

"Oh, stop it." Anna slapped them away. "Go meet your husband before he thinks you've stood him up."

"Right. I forgot about him. Call me if you need anything." Levi placed a kiss on each of the squirming twins' cheeks and then waved. "I'll be back by nine-thirty."

"Bye!"

The door slammed shut, and Anna was left with two bewildered-looking children watching her with saucer-round eyes.

"Auntie Anna," Lois said, lengthening the

words in a way Anna knew meant she was about to ask for something, "Can we go to the fair and get candy floss?"

"Yay, candy floss!" Ralph tugged on Anna's hand so forcefully that she barely had time to collect her purse before the kids were dragging her out onto the seafront. Anna squinted against the low sun and hoards of bodies — the final weekend before the kids went back to school, she'd wager, and the place was packed with tourists.

So packed, in fact, and so hectic to navigate with two children yanking her forward, that the store's keys were left forgotten on the counter inside, and Anna didn't so much as spare them a thought.

Thirteen

The door was already unlocked when Stevie slid the key into it the following day. It creaked open with ease against her weight, and icy panic seized her with both hands.

She almost didn't want to go any further.

Her feet crossed the threshold even when her mind screamed at her not to. Maybe she was mistaken. Maybe she had unlocked it and just hadn't heard it click. And then, when she found the store exactly as she had left it last night with the exception of the wooden dolls Lois and Ralph had no doubt played with, she thought maybe Anna had just forgotten to lock up — but that was okay. Nothing had happened.

She walked slowly to the counter, the cash register, and an involuntary, dread-drenched sob mangled in her throat as she brought her hands to her lips. The register was open.

And it was empty.

She checked the locked drawer underneath, where she kept larger sums and savings. Except it wasn't locked, though whoever had robbed the place had had the courtesy to shut it again.

Everything was gone.

Of course it was. Because the spare keys were splayed on the floor, not with Anna. She'd left them out for anyone to get hold of, and they had.

The sound of familiar footsteps tapping down the stairs, the ones Stevie heard every morning when Anna went to work, echoed from the hallway. Stevie waited until they reached the bottom before calling her.

"Anna?" She didn't know how she managed to keep her voice steady. Inside, a hollowness was eating her up, making her numb.

Anna pushed through the tangled beads and shells a few moments later, a small smile gracing her face. It soon fell when she noticed Stevie's forlorn features.

"What happened? Is it your dad? Is he okay?"

Stevie closed her eyes. No, it wasn't her dad. Not this time. He was ill with a chest infection, but he was getting the right treatment, and she'd left him snoring peacefully in his bed late last night.

"Did you lock up last night?"

"Ye…" Anna glanced to the empty cash register and the keys on the floor, face leaching of colour. "Oh, God. Stevie…"

Stevie clamped down another sob, though her chin wobbled as she leaned — fell — against the counter. *It could have been worse*, she tried to tell herself. *It's just money.*

But it was money Stevie didn't have. Money she needed for her mother and father and for herself. For the rent, which Deirde was expecting in *three days*.

"I didn't think," Anna whispered, placing her bag on the floor and inching cautiously across the dusty floorboards. "I had the twins and I didn't think."

"Did you not think or did you not care?" Unexpected anger bubbled in her chest, breaking through the void. She could only think of Anna breaking up with her, cold and detached, over Skype. Anna coming back without warning. Anna leaving the keys on the counter and the door unlocked. Maybe it wasn't fair, but Stevie didn't believe in fair anymore.

"Of course I cared! And I'll pay you back every penny, I swear."

Stevie shook her head in frustration, pressing the heel of her palm against her lids as though it might staunch the oncoming tears. It didn't. "I have rent due next week. Deirdre won't let me stay here if I keep delaying payments."

"I'll get you the money for her. I promise. It will be okay, Stevie." Anna reached an arm out, and Stevie recoiled, trying not to notice the pain twisting across Anna's features.

"Your promises haven't meant anything to me for a long time," Stevie breathed. "The shop is done. *I'm* done. I was hanging on by a thread and I don't think I can come back from this."

"No. No, Stevie, please don't talk like that."

But Stevie couldn't do it anymore. She

couldn't keep looking at the empty cash register and the keys lying on the floor and Anna's agony-stricken features. The shop was all she had that was hers. The thing she had chosen for herself, even if the outcome, the money, was to help her parents. And it had been invaded and taken away because of Anna's carelessness.

One night. She had asked just for one night where she could rely on someone other than herself. And it had ended in catastrophe.

She kicked the keys across the floor and pushed past Anna with fresh tears falling. And she left the shop without caring what came next. It hurt too much.

She couldn't do it anymore.

Anna didn't know what to do. There was no way she could think of to make this better. Stevie hated her. She would probably always hate her now, and Anna didn't blame her. She dragged her heavy feet and even heavier chest up the steps to her apartment after — pointlessly, now — locking up the store. Half of her wanted to run after Stevie, but there was no apology she could give that didn't sound weak and hopeless and pathetic in her own mind. It would take more than a few 'I'm sorrys' this time. A lot more.

Though Anna had unpacked last week, the

apartment felt cold and empty. Maybe coming back to Castell Bay at all had been her first mistake. Maybe everyone would have been better off if she'd stayed in Cardiff. Her mother. Her father. Stevie.

She could leave again. Find another job for a town or city she didn't particularly care about. She could pack it all up and never come back.

But she had done that before. It hadn't felt much better running away from the things she was afraid of, the things that hurt her. In the end, her heart would always be here. Home. Because it was where Stevie was. It had taken her too long to figure it out — or not long at all, if she thought of the devastation she'd felt the day she'd broken up with Stevie. And then after that, graduating with no loved ones in the crowd to support her. Moving to Cardiff permanently when she got her first internship. Coming home at the end of the day to microwave meals and a stifling quiet she'd filled with reality TV.

No. She wouldn't go back to that. She wouldn't run like a coward again. She would face her mistakes, show Stevie that it was different this time. That *she* was different this time. And if that did nothing to salvage them, which she doubted it would, she would just have to stick around and prove it like Levi had told her to.

Absently, her fingers ran across the creased and tattered spines of her bookcase. Were there books on how to fix things when you accidentally forgot to lock up your ex's shop and caused a break-in? From what she could remember of the film, Elizabeth Bennett *did* forgive Mr. Darcy for belittling her entire family. Surely that was worse.

But Keira Knightley had not looked as heart-wrenchingly devastated as Stevie had. Anna rubbed her eyes to try to forget the image, the teary eyes and the wobbling chin and the complete and utter disappointment.

Anna stilled when she came to the last book. *Persuasion*. She had taken it out of the car to keep it from getting anymore creases after Stevie had pressed the flowers between the pages. She'd wanted to preserve that memory the way the cornflower was preserved, so that if she ever did decide to read the book, she would find the smudged, intelligible ink on the exact pages Stevie used and remember.

Carefully, Anna slid it from the shelf and flicked through, stopping when she came to the vibrant blue cornflower petals flattened into the page. Tears pricked her eyes, and she didn't know why. She only knew that if there was anything in the world that could sum up Stevie, it was this. She found beauty in the ordinary and kept it safe and loved. With the wildflowers, with the seashells and driftwood she made into gifts, and with Anna. She had always kept Anna safe.

Anna closed the book and placed it back on the shelf, remembering only then that she was supposed to be at work. It was Friday. Village meeting day. And an idea began to form as she glanced at her watch. She might not be able to fix this, but she could try.

And she knew where to start.

Fourteen

Without security cameras or witnesses, the police hadn't been much help when Stevie went down to the station on Friday afternoon. They made it clear, in no uncertain terms, that unless a lead was plucked from thin air, the money wasn't coming back.

So, Stevie had gone back to the store, placed the closed sign in the window, and had not returned since. She didn't want to see all of her stock gone to waste, didn't want to imagine the space empty when she would inevitably have to clear it out.

She hadn't spoken to her mother about it yet. She didn't even have a plan for the future, other than the Etsy shop, which wouldn't provide her nearly enough income for two peoples' share of rent. How could she tell Bryn that? Thankfully, she'd left early this morning, so Stevie didn't have to. She'd been rattling aimlessly around the house since. It was too quiet, too empty, without her dad here.

At least it was until a heavy knock thundered at the front door. Stevie had no idea who it might be, but somehow, she hadn't been expecting

Levi. She hadn't told them yet either. Judging by the sympathetic gleam in their eyes that drowned her the minute she let them in, Anna had.

"I wasn't expecting you."

"You weren't answering my texts." The scolding was gentle and very un-Levi-like. They eyed her bedraggled appearance as though she was wearing a used bin liner and not just a very old, moth-eaten cardigan and paint-splattered dungarees. "Dear Lord. This is terrible. Why didn't you call me?"

"I don't look *that* bad." Stevie frowned, leading them into the living room. The armchair was sunken in from twenty years of her father sitting there each night, eating his dinner on his lap, and later, watching daytime television while his health deteriorated slowly.

Stevie didn't blame Levi, then, when they remained standing. "You look like you ransacked my great aunt's wardrobe."

Judging from the two times she'd met her, Stevie happened to like Great Aunt Mildred's fashion, but she only glared and crossed her arms. "I've had an awful week. I'm allowed to wear comfy clothes."

"These aren't comfy clothes. These are moping clothes."

"Well?" She shrugged. "I'm allowed to mope. Oh, and I'm alright, thank you for asking."

Levi softened and cast her a knowing, tight-lipped look. "I haven't asked if you're okay because

I already know you're not. Come here."

They extended their arms in offering, and Stevie sighed before falling into them. Her eyes stung with fresh tears as she inhaled the fresh scent of Levi's detergent, the same one the twins always smelled of, and Quentin. The one that reminded her of a family and warmth she'd never really had anywhere else. Not for a long time, anyway.

Because they *were* family. And Stevie regretted not calling Levi now. This is what she'd needed all along, not a stern-faced policeman asking her why she'd left the door unlocked twenty times over as though *she* were the perpetrator, and not her mother sighing every five minutes because she was constantly worrying about Jack.

No. She needed somebody to just hold her up for a little while. She needed her friends, her family. And thank God she had that in Levi.

"You don't mope, Stevie Turner," Levi murmured into her hair, holding her tighter. "You've never moped a day in your life."

"There's a first time for everything."

A chuckle hummed through their chest, vibrating against Stevie's cheek. "Well, I won't allow it. You're going to come to the market with Quentin and I, and you're going to share a big fat ice cream with the twins, and then we're going to have a picnic on the beach. How's that?"

"I don't know," she whispered wearily, pulling away and wiping her eyes. "I'm exhausted, honestly. I think I'm just going to go back to bed."

"Wrong answer." Levi began nudging her back into the hallway. "Go and put on one of your fancy summer dresses. It's warm outside. And brush your hair."

"*Levi*," she moaned. She really didn't think she could manage keeping herself together for a day, let alone playing the role of fun Auntie Stevie. "You're supposed to feel sorry for me and let me watch *Mamma Mia!* while feeding me chocolate. A good friend would."

"I'm not a good friend, my dear." They gave her a final push up the stairs.

"No, you're a monster." She traipsed up the stairs anyway, knowing that Levi wouldn't give in.

A few hours. She could be a non-weeping, non-broken person for just a few hours. She would have to be.

∞∞∞

The market was brimming with more people than Stevie had seen in a long time. There were more stalls than usual too, and a busker plucked a guitar melody in the corner. Had Stevie forgotten some grand Castell Bay holiday? She couldn't think of any that happened in September, but something was going on. Maybe it was the Queen's birthday. Marigold usually forced everyone to celebrate royal occasions.

"Auntie Stevie!" Lois shouted, tugging at her hand. Ralph held the other, Levi and Quentin trailing behind. "Candy floss!"

Indeed, Beth, who usually ran the sweet shop on the pier, was manning a candy floss machine, producing wonky pink clouds of sugar on wooden sticks.

Stevie turned to ask, "Is something happening today?"

"I don't know." Levi shrugged, brow raised as though they did, in fact, know. "Read the signs."

"What si — oh." It took her a moment to find them amongst all the chaos and bunting, but when she did, her heart stuttered in her chest and her legs stopped working. A gigantic poster had been strung onto the lamppost, reading: 'Save the Little Store of Driftwood' in neon blue.

Beneath, only slightly smaller: '50% of all proceeds will be donated to Castell Bay Hospice and Alzheimer's Association.'

"I don't understand," Stevie whispered, words catching in her throat and her fingers began to shake. "Did you two do this?"

"Nope," said Levi. "Our only job was to get you here. The woman you're looking for is over there."

They pointed to the corner stall where Stevie usually set up her own shop. Wall hangings and carvings still lined the tables, and behind them... Anna. She hadn't noticed Stevie yet, too busy selling something to... *Councillor Judith*?

This was surely an alternate reality, if Judith was splashing out on Stevie's stock.

"I think this is her way of saying she's sorry," Quentin spoke softly in Stevie's ear. "And that maybe she loves —"

"*Shh*!" Levi shushed. "You're stealing Anna's grand speech." They pushed Stevie along the cobbles. "Go on. Talk to her."

A lump throbbed in Stevie's throat, but her legs kept her drifting forward without permission. A dozen different townspeople patted Stevie on the shoulder or complimented her on the turnout as though she had anything to do with it. She could only smile falsely, attention unwavering from Anna.

She stopped in front of the stall, eyeing her own creations as though they were foreign objects. Anna's conversation with Archie, who sold ice creams in his usual spot, dissipated to nothing as Anna caught sight of Stevie. She licked her sea salt-chapped lips, rocking on her heels as Stevie tried to find... something. Something to say or do, something to ask.

But last time they'd talked, Stevie had blamed her for everything. What could she say? How could she pretend?

"Hello," Anna said finally. "Levi managed to get you here, then."

Stevie nodded, glad now that she had changed out of her comfy clothes and brushed her hair. "They did." An excruciating pause. "I... Did...

Did you organise all of this?"

"It was the least I could do." When Anna tucked her hair behind her ear, Stevie noticed her fingers were trembling. "I'm glad you made it."

"*How*?" Stevie couldn't help but blurt in awe, glancing around again at the packed village square. Marigold was by the burger van with her souvenirs. Paddy and his pies there. The twins were being handed two sticks of candy floss that were bigger than their heads and far more missha-pen. Levi and Quentin hovered by them, pretending not to be watching and doing an awful job of it.

"I mentioned what had happened at the vil-lage meeting on Friday," Anna shrugged. "That you were struggling after a robbery and, with your father in the hospice, needed some extra help. A lot of them didn't know Jack was so sick. They wanted to help, and I suggested a fundraiser."

"But that was two days ago." Not enough time to organise all of this.

"This community has always come together when it needs to."

"I don't know what to say." Stevie's voice was barely audible above the din of shoppers and music. She didn't know if Anna even heard her. "What about the bylaws? Why would the council let you do all of this when I'm not even supposed to use driftwood anymore?"

"I made a good case as to why your cre-ations are important. The bylaws have been lifted." Anna smiled gently, the corner of her eyes creasing against the bright, midday sun. She leaned across the table then, so that Stevie could make her out properly. "Look, I'm sorry. I'm so, so sorry, Stevie. You were right. I was careless and stupid and you deserve better. But I meant what I said. I'll pay you back every penny. Whatever I don't make up for today, I'll find another way to get. I swear. Just promise me you won't give up on the shop. The village needs it. We all do. Look at the lengths they'll go to save it."

Stevie did. She looked at the queue she was holding up and the big bowl marked 'Donations' at the edge of the table, stuffed with pennies and pound coins and five-pound notes. The village had come out here for her shop and her father today. Small businesses were selling their stock not for their own profit, but for hers. Because Anna had asked them to.

"I…" Stevie shook her head, at a loss for words. For the first time in a painfully long, dark time, she felt real, hot hope flickering in her stomach. Hope that she'd be okay. Hope that she wasn't alone and that she didn't have to carry everything on her shoulders. "Anna…"

There wasn't time for whatever it was she was about to say. Anna pointed to something behind her before she could get the words out, features brightening and wrapped in tendrils of sunlight, until Stevie didn't know where it ended and Anna began. "You have visitors."

Stevie whipped around — and almost collapsed on her shaky knees. Her mother was pushing Jack around the market in his wheelchair, townsfolk patting him on the back and holding conversation with him. It was sometimes difficult for him now he barely remembered faces, but he seemed happy enough today. And he wasn't sinking in that big hospice bed. He was out, breathing in the fresh air, smiling toothily.

Stevie would remember this moment for the rest of her life.

Bryn's face flashed with happiness when she spotted Stevie, and they approached quickly.

"You came." Stevie grinned, eyes filling with tears. "How?"

"Your Anna told us. We couldn't miss it, could we, Jack?" Bryn nodded appreciatively at Anna and then placed her hands lovingly on Jack's shoulders. He lifted one frail hand to squeeze his wife's. Even now, with everything in the world working against them, they could have these moments. Stevie knew they wouldn't last forever, but it was enough for today, for now, to see them both smiling and in love.

"No, no," Jack wafted off. "I want one of Paddy's steak and onion pies!"

"Dad." Stevie choked on a half-laugh, half-sob. "You're feeling better, then?"

"Well, we can't stay too long," Bryn answered for him, "but the nurse said a bit of fresh air wouldn't do him any harm. He might even be able to come home for a week or two soon."

Her smile grew, though she knew it would mean a lot of hard work caring for him again. But she would do it, just as she always did, if it meant spending time with a man she'd almost lost. "That's great news!"

"And don't worry," Bryn said. "They'll send round a nurse to do all the heavy lifting. You'll have plenty of time to focus on your shop, love."

Relief rattled through Stevie, though she resented herself for it. But it was time to accept that Jack needed more than Stevie and Bryn could give, and that was okay. She had done her best. She would always do her best.

And apparently, she had other things to do again now.

"Right, pie time," Jack ordered, nodding toward Paddy's stall. Bryn rolled her eyes and cast Stevie a final, beaming grin before toddling off with him.

Stevie turned back to Anna, still completely speechless and just about ready to burst apart for all the love and happiness and appreciation she felt. For the village, for her parents, for Anna. "You invited them. Thank you."

"It wouldn't be right not to," Anna said gently.

They locked eyes just for a moment, but it was enough that Stevie stopped breathing. Would she always feel like this when she looked at Anna, like the ground had slipped from under her and she was plummeting to somewhere unknown?

She scratched the back of her neck, suddenly very aware of the new customers trying to squirm past her. "Do you want me to take over?"

"No, of course not. You should enjoy it all. I can take care of the stall."

"Okay..." *We'll speak later*, formed on her lips but never left them, instead swallowed down by Stevie's disbelief — and fear. She was afraid. She was afraid that if she wasn't angry at Anna anymore, she would have to be in love with her again, and it was just so hard. Too hard.

She lowered her gaze, finding that there were only two windchimes left.

"I'll get you some more stock from the shop, then," she said quietly, and then wandered away before she got too lost in what all of this might mean.

Fifteen

Anna was not well-versed in manning a stall. She kept giving customers the wrong change and getting her hands tangled in the ribbons when she wrapped the delicate products up in brown paper. People asked her questions she didn't know the answer to. People asked if she sold things she'd never heard of before.

And with thoughts of Stevie distracting her, she was only getting worse.

"Quentin has got this covered for a while," Levi said, bumping her out of the way with their hip. "Stevie asked for help getting some more stock from the shop."

Quentin flanked her other side, batting her hands away when she tried to straighten out a wall plaque. "Go on. I have five years of retail experience under my belt."

"But —" Anna made to argue, but was soon cut off.

"Come on!" Levi urged, dragging her away from the market stalls and the noise. It was a welcome reprieve. Her feet were throbbing from standing in the same position on the uneven cobbles for hours on end, and she was sweating bullets in the midday sun. At least it was breezier down by the sea.

The bell above the door tinkled as Levi held it open for her, and she stepped in, finding Stevie piling more of her creations into a large bag. She glanced up when alerted by her presence, a small frown crinkling across her brows.

Anna didn't understand why until the door fell shut behind her, the sound of a lock clicking shut ringing out in the new silence. Levi had not come in behind her — and they had barricaded Anna and Stevie in the store.

"Levi!" Anna scolded, banging on the wood. "What are you doing?"

"You're not allowed out until you talk!" Levi's muffled voice drifted beneath the door. "*Properly* talk, not Anna-and-Stevie-talk, where you discuss anything other than your feelings for one another!"

"You must be joking," Anna muttered with a roll of her eyes. She turned cautiously back to Stevie to gauge her reaction to all of this.

She only scoffed and continued sorting the stock. "I despair. Why are we friends with them again?"

"I'm not anymore," Anna said, though it wasn't true. As obnoxious as Levi's meddling was, she did want to talk to Stevie. Perhaps now wasn't the best time for it, but she didn't seem to have much of a choice anymore.

"You do know I have my keys in here?" Stevie

shouted. "I can just *unlock* the door!"

"You'll have to get past me first," Levi replied, and Anna could hear the mischievous smirk in their voice.

With a sigh, Stevie abandoned her work and came out from the counter. "We could go out the back way."

They could… But Anna found her heart tugging for Stevie to stay. She didn't want to run away. Not again. She wanted to be here. She wanted to know if Stevie could ever forgive her. "I'd like to talk. If that's okay with you, that is."

Stevie chewed on her cheek. "Okay."

"I just… Well… " Maybe Anna should have planned this better. All of the words had been swimming around her head for days, but now she needed them, they wouldn't come. Where did she start? How could she find the right things to say? "Look, I just want to start by saying again how incredibly, utterly, immensely sorry I am for what happened. I *never* want to hurt you that way again. Never. I know it does —"

"I forgive you," Stevie interjected softly.

The words stunned Anna, lips parting. "You do?"

Stevie nodded. "Yes. I do. You made a mistake. I've done it plenty of times after a long day. Besides, you've done so much to fix it."

"Not enough," Anna whispered. "There'll never be enough to fix everything I've done to you, Stevie." She wasn't just talking about the shop anymore, and she hoped Stevie knew it, too. By the flicker of pain flaming across Stevie's face, she guessed she did.

"Well, not everything can be fixed."

"No. No, maybe not. I… I think some things don't have to be, though. Some things just take time to heal." Anna dared a step forward, breaths ragged. "And I'll wait for as long as it takes. I can be better this time. I know I can."

"Anna." It didn't sound like a protest. It sounded like a plea.

Anna didn't know what to do with it. "Tell me to shut up and I will."

She waited. Stevie didn't.

She let out a breath of relief and continued. "I can't ask you for anything. Not after all the pain I caused you. But… I can tell you the truth. I can tell you that I'm still in love with you. That I can't *stop* loving you. I don't think I ever will, and I don't think I ever want to."

Tears glistened in Stevie's eyes. She didn't move, didn't blink. Anna had never felt so raw, so bare, but she found it was a relief more than a burden to let herself be so vulnerable. After so long trapping herself, pushing all of those feelings down in the hopes something else, something easier, would fill her Stevie-shaped void… it was freeing to tell her now. Even if it was the only chance she ever got.

"I was so focused on my own pain for such a long time that I couldn't bear to think of how I must have made you feel. I know that you must doubt everything I say. That I don't deserve you. But I only feel right when I'm with you, Stevie. And living without you was dull and awful and if I could take it all back, I would.

"But I can't. I can only stand here now and tell you that I will never leave again. This is my home. *You're* my home. And I'll keep proving that I want to stay until you believe it again."

A sickening silence clawed through the chasm between them. Stevie finally blinked, and tears rolled down her pale, freckled cheeks. Anna could feel her own eyes stinging. But it was all out now. Everything she felt. Every regret she had. She didn't know if it would be worth a thing, but she'd tried. She would try again and again and again for Stevie. She would fight to get her back until she bled if it meant a second chance.

"I'm not the same person I used to be," Stevie said finally.

"I know," Anna said, because she did. She wasn't looking at Stevie through the hazy, rose-tinted lens of nostalgia and summers and adolescence. She was looking at her here, now: a woman who would pull apart every fibre of herself for the people she loved. A woman who laughed and cried and supported her friends and family. A woman who created beautiful things even when she was in pain. Auntie Stevie. Flower-pressing Stevie. The Stevie who had carried Lois across the beach with arms safe enough to fall asleep in. The woman who had defended Anna when Anna couldn't defend herself.

Like her creations, every part of her was beautiful, even the splintered parts and the parts she'd glued back together again. She was seashells strung on threads and driftwood carved into lighthouses, sun-bleached and salt-laced, and Anna loved her.

"Everything is complicated. My life… It's complicated."

"I know," Anna repeated. "So is mine. But isn't it easier when we manage it together?"

Stevie's throat bobbed as she shuffled, and Anna knew she was running out of excuses. She knew that if she just kept standing here, kept trying, Stevie would let her reach out eventually.

A shout from outside the door startled them both. Levi. "Have you kissed and made up yet?"

Anna shook her head, suppressing a smirk. Her attention remained on Stevie. "I can give you time if you want. If —"

But that sentence was never finished. Stevie reached Anna in two strides and kissed her with a ravishing, all-consuming hunger that left Anna's lips, her skin, feeling blistered and tingling and *right*. When her teeth grazed Anna's tongue, a moan fell from her throat.

"Those are definite kissing sounds!" Levi shouted, and then cheered. God only knew what passersby must have thought.

Stevie giggled, the sound light and tinkling

as the beads dangling in the threshold. She rested her forehead against Anna's, her fingers crawling along Anna's jaw.

"We need new friends," Anna said. "This one is scaring away the customers."

"I love you," Stevie breathed.

Anna readied herself to say it back, but the clicking of the lock again interrupted. The door swung open to reveal Levi, their hand splayed over their eyes. "Are we decent in here? It's just that I left the twins with Archie and I'm worried about how much ice cream they're about to consume."

"Yes, we're decent," Anna scoffed, pulling away only slightly to face them.

Levi lowered their hand reluctantly, their face splitting into a wide, dimpled grin at the sight of Anna and Stevie's still laced together. "My work here is done, it seems."

"Yes, and you're never having the keys to my shop again." Stevie snatched the keys from Levi and shoved them in her pocket. "Neither are you," she said to Anna in jest.

"That's very fair," Anna said.

"Okay. Must go and save twins from imminent brain freeze and tummy aches. I'll see you later." Levi blew them both kisses as they sprinted back up towards the village square.

Anna watched them go, shaking her head. "We need new friends," she repeated.

"I don't know." Stevie shrugged. "They could be worse."

She tilted her head into a kiss again, and Anna knew she would never get used to the way her spine tingled in response. It was short and sweet, and she pulled away too quickly upon realising that the stall had been left with Quentin.

"We should get back," she suggested.

They did, armed with bags of stock that were almost thrown to the floor when they reached the market and Anna caught sight of her father. She hadn't seen Daniel since the dinner, though she'd called him almost everyday while he stayed at his brother's to see how he was faring, and she had sent him a text invite for today. Apparently, the marriage was well and truly over and he was already looking into divorce lawyers — and Daniel was okay with that. It had been over for a long time, he'd said. Anna wondered if her parents might even be better apart. She could at least mend things with her dad, now, without the looming pressure of her mother.

"Hello, love!" Daniel greeted, gathering Anna into a bone-crushing hug. "Stevie," he greeted happily.

"Hi, Mr. Conway. I'll, er, leave you to it. Okay?" The question danced in Stevie's eyes.

Anna nodded reassuringly, squeezing her hand before Stevie returned to the stall.

"You two are going strong, then?" asked Daniel.

She couldn't help the soft smile that curled across her lips. "I think so, yeah. How are you?"

"Not bad at all. Have you..." Daniel fidgeted and cleared his throat. "Have you heard from your mum since...?"

"No." Anna hadn't. No phone calls, no visits, no apologies. She didn't want any either. Maybe in time, she'd be able to forgive her mother, but for now, her focus was on better things. Things that made her happy. It was liberating to finally be free of Jen's festering secrets. "You?"

"Not since I asked for a divorce. Better that way, though, I think. I hope you know I don't blame you for any of it, love. What happened wasn't your fault. Your mum never should have put you in that position."

"I hated lying to you," Anna admitted weakly. "I wish I'd have done things differently."

Daniel squeezed her shoulder gently. "Hey. No regrets. I've finally got you back, and that's more than enough for me."

"Love you, Dad." Anna flung herself into Daniel's arms again, eyes fluttering shut against the lines he drew on her back. Just like when she was a kid, before she'd had to hide things from him. Before she'd pulled away. She wouldn't do that again. Not with him, not with Stevie, and not with anyone else.

When she fell away, she found Daniel teary-eyed. He wiped his eyes with the cuff of his shirt-sleeve. "Love you too. Blimey. You know how to make a grown man cry."

Anna laughed. "You know, we're going for a

picnic later on at the beach. You should come."

"Oh, I wouldn't want to intrude."

"You wouldn't be," she said perhaps too quickly. But there was so much making up for lost time to do, and all she wanted was to finally be surrounded by everyone she loved again. "The more the merrier."

"Go on then," Daniel agreed. "I'll treat us all to some ice creams after, how's that?"

Anna felt like a kid again as he pulled her in and kissed her forehead — but that was okay. She would let herself be young and vulnerable again. She deserved to be. No more guilt and self-loathing.

They wandered back to the market that way, and Anna went straight back to Stevie. It was still bustling with people throwing their money at her, but Stevie still found the time to lift her gaze and mouth, "Okay?"

Anna grinned and snuck a kiss onto Stevie's flushed cheek. "Perfect," she murmured.

And it was. For once, it really, truly was.

About the Author

Rachel Bowdler is a freelance writer, editor, and sometimes photographer from the UK. She spends most of her time away with the faeries. When she is not putting off writing by scrolling through Twitter and binge-watching sitcoms, you can find her walking her dog, painting, and passionately crying about her favorite fictional characters. You can find her on Twitter and Instagram @rach_bowdler.